Lindsey Faraday and J.L. Brett are dangerously attracted to each other.

The kiss was light and over in a second, but J.L. knew he had wanted it to happen. And when he looked deeply into Lindseys's eyes, he saw in those mesmerizing blue diamonds the same acceptance of this crazy moment in time that they had been given.

Tiny wheat-colored lashes swept around the bottom of her eyes, and long, gently curved lashes defined their brilliance as she gazed up at him in silent surprise.

Without thinking, he brushed the back of his fingers across Lindsey's cheek, and she did not recoil, but he wondered what she would do if he tried to kiss her again.

Deciding he would be wise to retreat with his limbs intact, he straightened up, still holding her near, their eyes never leaving each other's. Hands on her waist, he held her lightly until her gaze lowered, in embarrassment, and the moment was broken.

Lindsey struggled to regain her composure, caught off guard by what had happened, confused that so simple a kiss could tumble her emotions and make her moan with pleasure. Or had that sound come from him?

Now safely on her feet and with her hair free, rational thought returned to her mind, but her cheeks were still warm from his touch and she realized: *I just kissed the enemy.* Her heart skipped a beat. *How could I have done that?*

KATHLEEN YAPP lives in Georgia with her husband, Ken; they have four children and six grandchildren. She is an accomplished writer of both contemporary and historical romances.

Books by Kathleen Yapp

HEARTSONG PRESENTS
HP70—A New Song
HP97—A Match Made in Heaven

Golden
Dreams

Kathleen Yapp

Heartsong Presents

To THE GROUP,
> Ron and Betty Jo Freeman,
> Stu and Aura Monfort,
> Bob and Betty Spicer,
> who shared a weekend in the mountains
>   with Ken and me,
> explored a gold mine and ate apple pie,
> laughed with us until we cried,
> and will be our dear friends forever.

A note from the Author:
I love to hear from my readers! You may write to me at the following address: **Kathleen Yapp**
Author Relations
P.O. Box 719
Uhrichsville, OH 44683

ISBN 1-55748-863-0

GOLDEN DREAMS

Cover illustration by Brian Bowman.

one

The click of a rifle being cocked stopped J.L. in his tracks.

He was about thirty feet inside the entrance to a gold mine, in the Laguna Mountains of southern California, and intense darkness hindered his vision of the ten-foot-wide tunnel in front of him. But he knew someone was there, with a gun, someone who could see him clearly silhouetted in the sunlight that streamed into the mine behind him.

Not moving, J.L. listened for a sound to tell him where the person was now, and he heard it—small rocks and gravel being crunched beneath the feet of that someone who was approaching him from the front, although it sounded like the sound was coming from behind him, too. Even though it was cool inside the mine, his heart speeded up and sweat exploded on the back of his neck.

Then he saw the rifle barrel, aimed at his chest, and his body stiffened. Dropping the envelope he was carrying, he quickly raised his arms and yelled, "Don't shoot!" But a bullet ripped from the gun, splaying the dirt and gravel behind him, and J.L. dove to his left, losing his Stetson, and scrunched himself against the shadowed, rocky wall of the mine.

He started breathing again after ten seconds when he felt no pain, saw no blood, and knew he wasn't dead.

"Are you all right?" a woman's frantic voice called out through the darkness.

J.L. stayed where he was, not about to be suckered into showing himself, even though the voice sounded genuinely concerned.

But when he saw her, not five feet from him, the Winchester

still pointing at him, he lunged, fiercely gripping the rifle and shoving it skyward at the same time his powerful arm circled her waist and yanked her against him with all the delicacy of a bull squashing a chicken.

The gun fell to the ground and he kicked it away, the barrel clacking loudly over rough dirt before it crashed into the opposite wall.

"Are you crazy?" the young woman gasped.

"Only when someone's using me as target practice," he growled through clenched teeth.

"I wasn't shooting at you."

"Really? Who else is in this tunnel?" He was there to talk with the mine's owner. How had he stumbled into World War III?

"There was a mountain lion behind you, but I missed him."

"Right," J.L. laughed scornfully, looking down into fierce, luminous eyes that challenged him and quickened his pulse.

"It's been attacking dogs and cattle in this county," she explained, wrestling to free herself from his viselike grip, "but so far he's eluded trackers."

"I didn't know California had mountain lions." J.L. relaxed his grip on her as he decided she wasn't all that dangerous.

"Over five thousand, and they're becoming more aggressive and losing their fear of humans because their habitat is being developed."

Her voice was low, and smooth, like rich cream, and he liked the sound of it. He also liked the sheen of her long, blond hair and the curve of her full lips.

Suddenly he let her go, wondering what a woman so beautiful, wearing dungarees and a green pleated blouse, was doing in so rough a place as a gold mine, carrying a loaded gun. "So you're a committee of one to catch this carnivore?" he asked.

She quickly stepped away from him, placed her hands on her hips, and shook her head. "Hardly, but this morning one of the men who works here told me he heard an animal, digging on Level Two. I brought the rifle, thinking I might find the cat, or some other animal, that had decided to set up house in this mine and wouldn't like the idea of being dislodged. When I heard the crunch of your boots, I came looking—"

"And found me."

"And the lion behind you."

J.L. let out a big sigh. Those were the other footsteps—pawsteps—he had heard. "Could we go outside?" he asked, leaning over to retrieve his cowboy hat, which he brushed off but kept in his hands. "I'm getting claustrophobic in here."

"Sure."

Picking up the rifle, Lindsey Faraday led the way out of the tunnel, her heart still pounding erratically. When she had first heard the sounds, she hadn't known whether it was a stranger in her mine who didn't belong there or the animal she hunted. All the men who worked for her had gone home for the day. Santiago, her foreman, was still in town. It was too late in the afternoon for tourists to be dropping by.

Finding two intruders in the mine had been a shock, but her daddy had taught her how to shoot when she was just a teenager, and she rarely missed when she aimed. She wasn't at all a hunter, but she did enjoy knocking tin cans off a fence behind the mine office. Today, all the years of practicing had paid off.

The cat she had seen must have been close to two hundred pounds, and there was little doubt in her mind that it had been looking for something to eat. Even though she hadn't killed it, she had scared it away and saved this man's life.

And what a man he was. Now that they were out in the sunshine she could see him clearly for the heart-stopping, big guy that he was, all six-feet-something, two-hundred-muscled pounds of him. She almost dropped the rifle from pure admiration.

The only word for him was rugged. From thick, unruly dark

hair the color of wet earth that surrounded a chiseled face that belonged on Mount Rushmore, to his broad shoulders and formidable chest that filled every inch of a blue western shirt, to his powerful legs encased in blue jeans. Rugged. Even his expensive but scuffed boots sent a message of strength.

Whoever he was, his hard, solid body reminded Lindsey of the rock walls of her mine, his voice of the deep shafts.

"Am I lucky to be alive?" he asked with a questioning look from intense, brown eyes behind pronounced lashes. He jammed the hat onto his head, leaving a shock of hair dangling across his forehead.

"I don't mean to brag, but I can hit a target at two hundred yards," she told him.

"You didn't hit the mountain lion."

"I scared him away."

"That's not the same as hitting."

"Look," she said, miffed at his ingratitude, "there were a few problems in between, namely the darkness and you."

"You took an awful chance."

There was no smile in his dark, assessing eyes, nor the defined creases down his cheeks, and his generous mouth pulled taut across a determined jaw made clear his annoyance at being shot at.

"I apologize if I scared you," she grumbled.

"More than scared. You took five years of my life."

"Which you might not have had if I hadn't pulled that trigger."

"Am I supposed to thank you?"

"That would be nice."

They stared at each other a moment, each recognizing in the other a stubborn streak that didn't give ground easily.

J.L. shrugged. "Then I thank you."

It irritated Lindsey that he didn't appreciate what she had done for him, but she wasn't about to get into a full-blown argument over it. "You were trespassing on private property, you know," she said.

"I have business here."

"And what might that be?"

From his serious expression, Lindsey guessed he was a man who always put business first. "I'm looking for Lindsey Faraday," he said.

She took a deep breath and let it out slowly, wondering what he wanted with her and already deciding that whatever he was selling, she didn't want any. They hadn't gotten off on even ground, which was too bad because she didn't like confrontations. Getting along was better.

"I am Lindsey Faraday," she told him, "and I really am sorry about what just happened."

J.L. stared. For the first time since he could remember, he was speechless. *She* was Lindsey Faraday? *She* owned the Lucky Dollar Mine? He had been expecting a tough old gal with stringy gray hair, skin like sandpaper, baggy clothes, and a voice that could skin a mule at twenty paces.

Lindsey Faraday was a far cry from that. With the sun shimmering through her long, honey blond hair that hung straight and floated behind narrow shoulders, there was a childlike innocence about her that was enhanced by intelligent, diamond blue eyes and a petal-small mouth.

She was tall and slender, and made him think of undulating leaves on a weeping willow tree, and words to describe her came easily to mind: memorable, feminine, intriguing. Warm. She had felt warm in his arms, the very opposite of the cold, hard steel of the gun she had been carrying.

"I'm pleased to meet you, Miss Faraday," he managed to say without his voice cracking like a lovestruck teenager's, and he whipped his hat off his head, gave her a quick bow in respect, and stepped back, trying to keep his eyes from wandering over every exquisite inch of her. He considered himself a gentleman, after all, who did not put undue importance on a woman's physical appearance. What she was inside—her character, her motivations, her intelligence, her love of God—those were more important than superficial beauty.

"Let me introduce myself," he went on. "I'm Jonathan Logan Brett and I'm an attorney from San Diego." He smiled just enough to produce two adorable dimples in those otherwise hardened cheeks, and Lindsey couldn't help smiling in return as she shifted the rifle from her right hand to her left and put out her hand to meet his, which he took and kept in his.

What kind of lawyer wears a black Stetson, leather-corded bola, and boots big enough to squash a cobra? she wondered, noting also the robust and tanned look of him that told her he spent as little time as possible indoors, behind a stuffy desk in some glassed-in office.

"I have business to discuss with you," he said, releasing her hand, which allowed Lindsey's heartbeat to return to normal …almost.

"Business?" she asked.

"Yes. On the floor of the mine is a paper you need to see, Miss Faraday, which I dropped when I put my hands up and requested, politely I thought, that you not shoot me."

Lindsey grinned. "Which I didn't."

"That's true." His eyes glanced at the rifle she still held. "If I get that paper from the mine, you won't shoot me will you?"

"Not unless you prove to be more dangerous than that mountain lion," she teased back.

"I'm a kitten," he promised, and Lindsey knew that was pure fallacy. Everything about the man was full grown and disquieting: the way he stood, the rumble of his voice, the set of his shoulders, the way he looked at her that made her skin tingle in the nicest way.

She watched him stride across the rough and graveled ground and disappear into the mine, her mind finally focusing on what kind of business a lawyer from San Diego might have with her.

two

When J.L. returned, Lindsey expected him to give the paper to her. Instead, he said, "Can we talk this over in your office?"

He looked around the hilly, rather barren grounds for such a place, and Lindsey felt a rush of apprehension. *Does he think I'm going to need to sit down after I read this?* She could not imagine what serious business he could have with her. She was scrupulously up to date on all her bills, wasn't being sued by anyone, and, as far as she knew, there was no long-lost relative who had recently died and left her a million dollars...unfortunately.

She studied J.L. Brett, and tried to think the best. *Maybe he's drumming up business...wants me to make out a fancy will or open the mine for public investment.*

As if reading her mind, J.L. tapped the envelope. "You'll know when you read this. It will take only a few minutes, and I'll be glad to answer any questions you might have."

With a nod yes, Lindsey pointed behind her to a dilapidated wooden square of a building with a tin roof, about forty feet away. "My office is over there."

As J.L. looked at the building, Lindsey began seeing it through his eyes. It wasn't much, just some timbers that seemed to lean into the mountain behind it and had seen better days...a hundred years ago maybe. There were a few windows, not too clean, she realized with a dash of guilt, and a metal smoke-stack that was bent and had also seen better days.

Some manzanita bushes, but no flowers, grew across its front, and two huge oak trees guarded either side, their branches spreading over the top of the office and embracing far enough

above the roof not to be in danger of catching fire from way-
ward sparks released from the potbellied stove within.

He might as well know I don't go in for frills, she thought,
and started walking toward the building. J.L. fell in beside
her, his gait smooth and powerful, she noticed, like a cougar
sure of its territory.

There was an aura of manliness about him that exuded self-
confidence. He gave the impression of a man who knew who
he was, what he wanted in life, went after it, and most always
got it. But what was he after now?

She liked the fact that he had not been ashamed to admit
that he had been afraid when she was shooting at him. And he
didn't seem to be arrogant, just determined.

As they strode toward the office, he didn't make small talk,
but his eyes swept over the terrain, taking in everything around
him. Idle curiosity, or was it more? she wondered.

In the one-room mine office of dusty file cabinets and tech-
nical equipment scattered around the floor and on rickety tables,
he gave Lindsey the envelope and she took from it the single
sheet of paper and began reading it.

J.L. watched her, for reaction, and his pulse quickened as he
realized he was attracted to her. She was more than interesting, more than beautiful. She was…intriguing. Why was she
here, in this rough, bleak place—a delicate rose in the midst of
rubble?

She was almost an enigma, a woman who looked like an
angel but could shoot a powerful weapon of destruction. A
woman who certainly would win men's attention, yet was sepa-
rated from them by a life's work in a remote mountain.

Even the scent of her was different: not that of expensive
French perfume but of…what? Yes, talcum. That white, soft
powder that goes on every baby's bottom and soothes. On her
it smelled every bit as intoxicating as if it cost a hundred dollars an ounce. *Intoxicating. That's what she is,* he thought,
starting a mental list of her attributes that already included

intriguing, stunning, and intelligent.

His admiration soon turned to concern as he saw the expression on Lindsey's face range from disbelief to anger. He knew he had a fight on his hands.

"This is garbage!" she declared, her eyes flashing fire when she looked up at him. She crumpled the letter in a ball and tossed it at him.

"Excuse me?" He grabbed the paper before it fell to the floor.

"Garbage," she repeated. "Ridiculous. Untrue." She strode behind a gray metal desk and threw herself into a sturdy, straight-backed chair.

"Why do you say that?" J.L. questioned. He had not expected that reaction to the facts. Hooking a well-used wooden chair near the desk with the toe of one boot and deftly turning it around so it was facing Lindsey, he sat down in it and wondered just how much she really knew about the running of the mine. She probably had a business manager. He would talk to him.

With undisguised animosity, Lindsey stared at him. "My daddy, Mr. Brett, would have never borrowed thirty thousand dollars and then not repay it."

J.L. met Lindsey's stare with conviction in his own. "My client has a Note and Deed of Trust, found in the papers of her recently deceased mother, that says William Faraday, your father and then owner of the Lucky Dollar Gold Mine, borrowed a great deal of money from her in 1985 and never paid it back."

"No, he didn't."

Add stubborn to the list, J.L. thought.

"And I know that," Lindsey went on, "because we worked together for many years before he died, running this mine." The words were sharp, like bullets exploding from the rifle she had been carrying. "He would have told me if he had had to borrow that much money."

While J.L. wondered just what she meant by "worked

together…running this mine," he watched her with the practiced eye of a court attorney used to determining if people were lying under examination. Lindsey Faraday looked straight at him with eyes that did not blink. Her breathing was heightened and her small, narrow hands were locked together on the desk in front of her, although he was sure they would like to be pummeling his chest instead.

Still, he could swear she was telling the truth, as she knew it. But she was wrong about her father. She had to be.

"The Lucky Dollar was used as collateral," he told her.

"Impossible."

Stubborn and tenacious, he expanded the list of her qualities that had started out loftily the first moment he had seen her but was deteriorating into more negative ones as she refused to accept the truth of what he was telling her.

"Do you have proof the Note was repaid?" he asked.

"I don't need proof for a loan that was never made."

"Yes, you do."

Lindsey watched J.L. sit forward and slowly, meticulously, unfold the letter from his law firm, pressing out with long, wide fingers, lightly sprinkled with the same dark hair that covered his head, the creases she had made when she had wadded it up. There was danger in his silence, in the methodical way he worked on the letter, like a wild animal skillfully and patiently stalking its prey. Even so, Lindsey was not prepared for the strike.

"If you don't repay the loan voluntarily, Miss Faraday," he said gently, but with his eyes locked to hers, "the Lucky Dollar will be sold to raise the money."

"Foreclosure?" she screamed. Every muscle in her body went taut, and she leaped to her feet. "How dare you come onto my property and tell me I'm about to lose the most precious thing in my life. My father and I struggled for years to make the Lucky Dollar produce enough gold and silver to provide us with a comfortable living, and no two-bit cowboy lawyer is going to change that."

J.L. stood up, too, surprised at the vehemence of her challenge. He was used to people getting angry with him over legal matters, and he knew how to control his own reactions when they did. Even name calling didn't push him over the edge, because when a man's temper is lost, so is his ability to make the kind of decisions that win cases.

Now, however, this ravishing, stubborn, exasperating woman was stirring conflicting emotions in him: he wanted to insist she just do as he said, pay the money, and get it over with. He also wanted to tell her he was sorry and ask her out to dinner.

"Our discussion is over, Mr. Brett!" Lindsey declared before J.L. could decide which direction to take and, walking out from behind the desk, she strode deliberately across the room and was almost past him before he reached out and captured one arm.

"I'm not leaving here, Miss Faraday, until I know what you intend to do about this."

She whirled to face him and he gave her just as fierce a look as she was giving him. "Is there someone else I should talk with?" he asked. "Someone who handles your business affairs?"

He knew he had made a tactical error the minute the words were out of his mouth, as temper raged in her eyes. "So, Mr. Brett, you're a chauvinist as well as a bully."

J.L.'s mouth dropped open.

"No one knows the details of this mine more than I do," she informed him hotly with an determined lift of her chin. "I need to look through my father's papers again."

Is she stalling or desperate? J.L. pondered, and he saw signs of both in her fiery blue eyes, watching him expectantly for his answer, a determined woman, resolved not to give up a large sum of money without a fight, which he certainly understood and applauded. He also saw a flash of desperation, like a cornered wild animal not sure how to escape. He wasn't quite able to figure her out, but he would have to if he were going to secure for his client what was rightly hers and what she so urgently needed.

"All right," he said finally, as though he were commuting a death sentence, knowing the power he had over her made him number one on her shoot-at-dawn list. "Three days to come up with proof of repayment."

"Which is what?"

"A Full Reconveyance. But the fact that no such document was ever filed with the County Recorder, and my client still has the Note and Deed of Trust—"

"I'll look anyway," Lindsey insisted. *Time,* she thought. *I need time.* Not that she thought that would do any good, because when her father died she had thoroughly gone through everything of his, and there had been no evidence that such a serious transaction had taken place. But how was she going to convince J.L. Brett and the client he represented of that?

She spun on her heels and, straightening her shoulders, walked to the door and opened it with a flourish, allowing the bright California sunshine to burst into the room. She was dismissing him. She hoped he realized that. She never wanted to see him again, despite his rugged, handsome face and deep, rumbling voice. She was getting more agitated by the moment, and who could blame her? She was being threatened.

She wasn't expecting him to move with the force of a tornado across the room, and stop so close to her that she had to put her head back to look up at him. He pushed the door shut.

"Are we going to settle this peaceably, Miss Faraday?"

Each word was punctuated clearly with the warning that they had better do just that, but Lindsey stood her ground against his formidable size and scowling eyes. "Probably not," she retorted, "since your client wants what is mine."

"What is hers."

"According to you."

J.L. Brett shook his head emphatically. "According to legal documents."

"That I have not seen yet." Lindsey knew she had a temper. It was something she wanted the Lord to help her eliminate, now that she was born again. Though she had a new life in Christ, just a few weeks old, sometimes the old life roared into action and she struggled against it, like she was doing now, standing toe to toe with this maverick lawyer who wouldn't take no for an answer. While she had never totally lost control with another human being, J.L. Brett just might be the first.

"I shall be happy to show you those documents," he pressed.

"Another day, perhaps." She yanked open the door. Her voice had risen ten decibels in ten seconds.

"They're in my truck." He pushed the door closed.

"Then go get them!"

When Lindsey saw every muscle in his body expand and his jaw turn to stone, she suspected that J.L. Brett was not used to taking orders. And, when a hand big enough to crush a cantaloupe tore the old door open with such force the old hinges ripped from the frame, she knew it.

He stood there, stunned, holding up the huge piece of wood with one hand. Then, with a grunt of frustration that was actually a growl, he let the door crash to the floor and stormed down the path toward the parking lot, nearly running into Santiago Ramirez, her foreman, who was coming toward the office.

Santiago gave Lindsey a concerned look and she knew he was seeing flaming cheeks and one angry woman.

"Trouble, boss?" he asked tentatively.

"No more than a hurricane, flood, and earthquake all put together," she declared, wishing she had something to throw at the departing figure of J.L. Brett. In less than fifteen minutes the man had threatened her livelihood, destroyed the door of her office, and made her more furious than any person she had met in her life. "Add to that tidal wave."

Then she kicked the door, and howled as her foot started to hurt.

three

When J.L. opened the door off his burgundy pickup truck, he nearly tore it off. Hurling himself into the driver's seat, he yanked a yellow legal pad from his leather briefcase and a gold ball point pen from the pocket of his shirt, and scrawled across the top of the paper in huge, bold letters, LINDSEY FARA-DAY. Down the left side he put, "stubborn, temperamental, uncooperative," saying the words through his teeth as he wrote them, then added "defensive" and "unrealistic" with a flourish.

Leaning over the steering wheel, he stared at the list, and took a half-dozen deep breaths before he felt under control again.

"Why did I let that woman get to me?" he asked himself out loud. Tossing the legal pad onto the seat beside him, he slumped back and closed his eyes, feeling like he had been caught in a revolving door that was still going around.

He had lost his temper, which was unprofessional, immature, and against his Christian conscience, and which certainly had not persuaded that feminine ball of fire that his client's claim was legitimate.

Jamming the pen back into his pocket, J.L. reached inside his briefcase and took out an envelope that held copies of the Note and Deed of Trust his client had found in her mother's estate. Looking at it he said, "I hope your contents do a better job of convincing Lindsey Faraday than I did." Then he got out of the truck and, with giant and purposeful steps, he walked back on the path toward the office, fully expecting the beautiful Miss Faraday to meet him halfway and with her rifle aimed at his chest.

But she didn't. She was still in the office, talking with a burly Hispanic man who was under six-feet tall but had the shoulders of an ox connected to the body of a bull.

When J.L. walked in, both Lindsey and the man, whose hair was jet black and wiry and whose deeply lined face told the story of a hard life, fixed dark looks on him that made him feel about as welcome as a rattlesnake at a picnic.

"I have the papers you wanted to see," he said, holding up the envelope and feeling the acute embarrassment of an adult who had behaved childishly.

Neither Lindsey nor the man spoke, nor moved.

Clearing his throat, J.L. went on, with true sincerity, "I'm sorry about the door."

The man looked down at the wood on the floor.

Lindsey Faraday stepped forward and, to J.L.'s amazement, gave him a tiny smile as she took the envelope and said, "I apologize, too. Getting angry never solves a problem."

J.L. nodded his head in agreement. "I'll pay for the damage."

"You don't have to. The door was old; we've needed another."

"I'd feel better if I did," he insisted gently.

For a long moment they looked at each other, uncertain if this was a truce, then Lindsey said, "All right."

She gestured toward the big man beside her. "This is my foreman, Santiago Ramirez."

J.L. stepped forward and thrust out his hand. "J.L. Brett." The other man hesitated but gave him one of the strongest handshakes he had ever received. A warning, no doubt, that Lindsey Faraday had a protector. "I'm an attorney from San Diego," J.L. clarified.

"That so?"

The look he received was a questioning one, and just short

of a scowl, and J.L. had the feeling that the man had not been told about the "situation." He wondered why not.

"So, you run the mine for Miss Faraday," J.L. said in supposition.

Lindsey frowned and Santiago chortled, the lines around his eyes and mouth softening. "No one runs nothin' for Miss Lindsey, señor. She, and she alone, keeps this mine going."

J.L. cocked his head and looked at Lindsey. "I see."

Pride flashed back at him from bright blue eyes and then Lindsey turned to Santiago and said, "You'd better check out that jump hole on Level Nine tomorrow. The timbers around it are starting to rot." She gave him a warm smile that J.L. wished were for him.

"Will do, boss. Did you find an animal in the mine when you checked it out today?"

The starting of a grin turned up Lindsey's mouth. "Yes and no, Santiago." She glanced at J.L. and he knew she was talking about him. He had never been called an animal before and he decided he and the lady mine owner needed to get a few things straight. Insulting him was not going to get her debt cleared.

Lindsey's attention was back with her foreman. "The mountain lion was there."

Santiago drew in a sharp breath. "On Level Two?"

"No, he wandered into the entrance, just behind Mr. Brett." Now she did grin. "I thought they were together at first."

Very funny, J.L. thought.

"I shot at him, but missed, and he got away."

The foreman's forehead deepened into a frown. "He might return, especially if he's been in the mine before. There was another strike last night, over at Miller's ranch. One calf dead, another maimed."

"Oh, no," Lindsey cried.

"Could be the same cat."

Lindsey nodded and J.L. felt the hairs on the back of his neck stand up. He could have been a victim, too, if this woman he was battling hadn't been there with a rifle.

"I'll tell the boys to keep an eye open for him," Santiago said. "The authorities think he might be a 'transient.'"

"What's that?" J.L. asked.

"A lion newly on its own, twelve-to-eighteen months old, no longer hunting with its mother, needing to establish a territory of its own," Lindsey explained. "Let's keep a lookout for 'scrapes,'" she said to her foreman.

Before J.L. could ask the question, Santiago answered, "That's a no trespassing sign a lion leaves around his home range...usually a pile of debris he's urinated on to warn off others."

Lindsey patted his arm. "Thanks for telling the boys about this, Santiago."

"Sure, boss." He glanced over at J.L. then back to Lindsey. "Will you be all right?" he asked her.

"Just fine, thanks."

"Okay."

He left the room with the force of a small storm, the old wooden floorboards vibrating under his weight, and J.L. muttered, "Interesting man."

"That he is," Lindsey agreed. "He's worked at this mine for over thirty years and is invaluable to me."

"And protective." He moved closer to her.

"Always." She stepped back.

"But you're the boss." It was a statement rather than a question and Lindsey was glad he understood that fact. In his eyes she saw respect and her fierce resentment of him softened.

When a warm smile from him drifted over her, weakening her knees, she walked briskly to the potbellied stove that had been there as long as the mine had, she suspected, and closed the door that didn't really need closing, but she did it anyway.

It was something to do to keep her away from J.L. Brett, to quiet the tremor of her hands, to distract her mind from this compelling lawyer who stirred her up, shortened her breath, and made her forget the real reason he was there.

That this tall, muscled, all-American male watching her now with growing interest should make her heart flutter, infuriated her. He was threatening her with the loss of her golden dream. He insulted her with his stubborn insistence that her father had been negligent in fulfilling a contract. He exasperated her with the certainty that he would not go away until the problem was solved, probably to her detriment.

So why was she attracted to him?

Of course she recognized how good looking he was, how developed and manly his body was. Certainly she had to admit he had dark, compelling eyes, and a strong mouth that would thrill a woman with its kiss. Undoubtedly he was intelligent and successful. Beyond argument he was a lethal combination of brains and brawn, sensuality and sensitivity. She wasn't stupid, or made of ice, after all.

She was, however, a woman who did not think a lot about men in "that" way, for her life had always been focused on the mine, and the dream she had shared with her father to find the Mother Lode.

Living 4200 feet up in the mountains, with mostly tough old miners and a few stray dogs for company, she had been somewhat isolated from many of the activities that other young girls grew up with. But she had never minded. Her father, and the Lucky Dollar, had been her whole world.

She had always expected to fall in love someday, get married, and have a family, but the men she had met around town and at university had shied away from a woman whose passion was a gold mine in a remote mountain.

She couldn't help it. The mine was, indeed, her passion, her love, always there, always demanding but faithful, always holding out to her the promise of even more satisfaction to come. And it was enough for her, or had been, until two months ago, when two major events entered her life: she became a Christian and met a man who wanted to marry her.

"How did you come to run this gold mine?" J.L. asked, interrupting her thoughts as he eased himself down on one corner of her desk, his hands laced together casually in front of him, one leg dangling, giving the appearance of his belonging there, in her office, on her desk.

Lindsey fought to overcome emotion with reason. The man was not interested in her; he wanted to know about the mine. He wanted to know the whereabouts of the thirty thousand dollars that he insisted belonged to his client.

Stabbing him with a look of impatience, she said, "I really don't have time to chitchat about my personal life, Mr. Brett," and she took out the papers he had brought her and she started to examine them.

But he slid off the desk and came over to her and laid his large hand on her small one, stopping her from reading them.

J.L. didn't want her to look at the copies of the Note and Deed of Trust that would prove his case. Not yet. They would ignite her ire again. For just a few minutes, he wanted to talk to her calmly, hear the melodic rhythm of her contralto voice, and have her smiling at him rather than regarding him coldly as the enemy-of-the-month.

She aggravated him one minute and fascinated him the next with her combination of intelligence and naïveté, and he wished he were getting to know her under any other circumstance than what he was. "Please tell me about you and the mine," he urged her. "I really would like to know."

"It isn't a very exciting story," she began, moving away from him. "I was eight years old when my daddy brought me to this mine. He was a successful stockbroker then, but gave it up to pursue a new life. To find the Mother Lode was his dream, and is now mine. I've grown up here, among crusty miners who'd rather work, for far less than they're worth, than make twice as much doing something else."

Her eyes filled with passion. "Mining gets in your soul, Mr. Brett. It becomes something you *have* to do." She stared at him. "Can you understand that?"

"Of course. That's how I feel about my work. As long as there are people being exploited, held down, kept from their rights and freedoms, I want to represent them."

"For a staggering fee, of course," Lindsey quipped.

J.L.'s eyes narrowed at the slur. "Believe it or not, I don't take advantage of people needing help. Winning a case for someone who can't win on his own gives me tremendous satisfaction."

"And is this client you currently represent one of those poor unfortunates who needs your expertise to win her her rights and freedoms?"

"Oh, yes. She needs the money your father borrowed."

"Allegedly borrowed," Lindsey corrected, deciding that was enough small talk for the day and she held the papers up and ran her eyes over them.

They were copies of the originals, as she had thought they would be, but they looked authentic enough. Her thoughts dashed to and fro looking for answers, frantic, as though she were being sucked into a whirlpool from which there was no escape.

She still clung to the belief that her father would never have left the mine in such jeopardy, and her loyalty was fierce, so she would fight hard to prove it justified.

Thirty thousand dollars. She almost laughed out loud. It might as well be thirty million. She didn't have either.

She looked up at J.L. and said firmly, "I suggest you talk with your client again, Mr. Brett, because these documents cannot be true."

"And I suggest you look through your father's papers again, Miss Faraday," he countered firmly.

Lindsey gave him a long look. He was so sure of himself, of his legal case, so smug and unbending. But he was wrong. She knew he was. She, after all, knew what kind of man her father had been.

"You gave me three days to prove my case," she reminded him pointedly.

"That's right."

"And I give you three days to be sure your client is not deceiving you."

J.L. expulsed a breath. "Why can't you see reason?"

"Oh, I do, Mr. Brett. And I just hope you can, too, because I guarantee you're going to have the fight of your life on your hands before you foreclose on my mine!" She promised this with all the sweet menace of one person handing another a lighted stick of dynamite, burning an inch from the end.

Turning away from him, she walked over to the open doorway, wanting him to understand that their conversation was ended. He followed her.

"You could make this a whole lot easier on all of us," he said, standing close to her, "if you'd just cooperate."

"How? By giving you what's not yours?"

His eyes narrowed, but he walked away without another word, and Lindsey wished the door were still intact so that she could slam it on him.

four

The first thing J.L. did when he got out to his truck was to take out his list on Lindsey Faraday and underline the words stubborn and temperamental. Then he added "sassy."

But when he started to put the yellow tablet back in his briefcase, he paused, then wrote on the opposite side of the page, LOYAL. He looked at it a long time and thought how lucky William Faraday had been to have a daughter who believed in him so much.

He wrote the word "beautiful," too, but the letters were small.

Three days, J.L. thought. *I'll see her again in three days,* and he was definitely glad he would, despite their tempestuous beginning and knowing that the skirmishes weren't over yet. For personal reasons as well as professional, he wanted to be with her.

She was different from any woman he had known, not just because she was trying to make it in a business dominated by men, but because she was a striking contrast between courageous and vulnerable, hard and soft. She was irritating and antagonistic, but he had also seen moments of lightheartedness and caring. He wanted to know her better.

As he headed his truck south and west toward San Diego, she stayed in his thoughts, like a romantic sonata, and he wondered what it would be like to go out with her. What would they talk about? What interests might they share?

Then he chuckled softly. "Right, Brett. I'm sure the lady is going to walk into the arms of the very man who has depleted her business by thirty thousand dollars."

Yet, he believed he could win her, because one of his strengths was the power of persuasion. If he could move juries and judges to his way of thinking, certainly he could convince this stubborn, tenacious, temperamental, uncooperative, defensive, sassy woman to share a pizza with him on a Friday night.

So, he decided, with a big sigh, *I'll ask her out, but not until this legal problem is settled. It wouldn't be ethical to do it sooner.*

He began to whistle, something he rarely did, and he smiled, knowing he would win this case against Lindsey Faraday, even though, for a while, they would be adversaries, a situation he did not want, but could not avoid. The real challenge would come afterward, in turning an adversary into a…friend.

❧

J.L. pulled into the downtown parking lot across from the eleven-storied building where his law practice was located, got out of the truck, and walked briskly across the busy street. The fresh air felt good. He would take it over air-conditioning any day, just as he would find almost any reason to be out of doors instead of inside.

His thoughts of Lindsey, as he strode through the gleaming lobby of his building with its marbled floor and brass accoutrements, were whether or not she could actually pay the money owed his client. There was certainly no doubt that she didn't want to pay and that she would fight him all the way to keep from paying.

The heavy elevator door closed and he pushed the button that would take him to the top floor. His research into the Lucky Dollar had revealed a gold mine that was still bringing in enough gold and silver to support its owner and a few employees, but to J.L.'s personal observation, the mine and its environs hadn't looked all that prosperous.

Still, he remembered reading that there remained more gold in those mountains than was ever taken out in its heyday and up to the present.

I wonder if she pays her employees dirt and keeps the big bucks for herself, he pondered as the door of the elevator silently slid open on his floor and he stepped out into a gargantuan reception area where his dusty boots sank into plush, forest green carpet and where the heavy woods and beveled glass were every bit as impressive as the tall man who walked among them.

Didn't she tell me herself that her miners worked for far less than they were worth? He allowed himself one last thought of her before he approached the moon-shaped walnut reception desk standing on a white alpaca rug.

"Almost time to go home, isn't it, Mrs. Larson?" he addressed the attractive, middle-aged receptionist who was busy at her desk, examining several envelopes of airline tickets. Her ivory, double-breasted suit and stylishly smooth brown hair added another touch of elegance to the already stunning surroundings.

She looked up at him and smiled broadly. "Yes, sir, it is about that time. Has it been a good day for you?"

He had been gone since early morning but knew that between Mrs. Larson and Heather Davenport, his executive secretary, the office couldn't be in more capable hands.

"It was an…unusual day, Mrs. Larson, but good," he answered, as all other business he had conducted paled in comparison to his experience with Lindsey Faraday at the Lucky Dollar Mine.

"I'm happy to hear that, sir. All's right with Brett and Associates, too."

"As I knew it would be. Is Mr. Packard on his way to Chicago?" he asked, looking at the airline tickets she held in her hand and referring to his newest associate, a recent graduate of the Harvard Law School.

"Tomorrow. I have his tickets here."

"How long will he be gone?"

"Two days."

"That should wrap up the case."

In the law firm of Brett and Associates, there were four associates, three men and a woman, all from different parts of the country and each specializing in a different field of law from civil and criminal cases to corporate and tax situations, from handling sensitive business for the rich and famous of all southern California to solving the dilemmas of the most humble of working people.

J.L. was the maverick amongst them, preferring the "unusual" cases, the ones that espoused a cause or were for people or groups who could not afford the high price of a competent attorney. In truth, it was the associates who brought revenue to the firm.

Turning down a hallway, he entered his secretary's office, on the other side of which was his own office.

Heather Davenport was there, as usual, working diligently at her desk, a gorgeous, dark-haired woman whose immaculate appearance and competent manner matched her skills as a Professional Secretary. In her late twenties, Heather was a college graduate with a major in English, was logically minded, dedicated, unemotional, and kept J.L.'s business running smoothly at all times. She was invaluable to him.

She was also in love with him, a fact he knew and regretted because his feelings for her involved only respect for her skills as a secretary and a general liking because she was easy to work with.

Some of his friends thought he was crazy for not dating her, but he was not about to get into those murky waters, mixing business and pleasure.

Because of Heather's careful attention to the day-to-day detail of his practice, he was free to involve himself in other areas, being a man who had learned early that much of a business's success could be the result of having talented secretaries.

"Good afternoon, Heather," he greeted her cheerfully,

noticing the strong scent of her perfume that he had never liked. He much preferred the gentle hint of Lindsey Faraday's talcum.

"I'm glad you're back, Mr. Brett," she enthused, jumping to her feet and following him into his office. "You have messages."

"Fire away." With a circular toss of the wrist, he threw his Stetson toward a large Remington bronze of "The Cowboy," where the hat landed square on the horse's head. J.L. smiled. "What's the most important?" he asked over his shoulder, dropping his briefcase onto a green three-seater couch. He went to a small niche in the corner where he opened a nearly hidden refrigerator and took out of it an old-fashioned sarsaparilla in a dark brown bottle. He was addicted to the stuff, but only if it was icy cold. Taking a long, thirsty drink, while thumbing through some papers on his desk, he listened to Heather's precise recitation.

"Senator Billings called about that government fraud case you're handling. The television station wants to set up a time tomorrow afternoon for your interview about the Flores trial. Joe Blyden over at the courthouse wants you to represent his daughter who's being sued for sexual harassment."

J.L. stopped rummaging and looked up, surprised. "*She's being sued?*"

"Yes, but Joe said it's a smokescreen. The man wants her job and can't get it any other way than to get rid of her first."

"I'll call Joe later. Anything else?"

"Your mother wants your advice on a birthday present for your father. Next Wednesday's the big day."

"Okay. I have something in mind."

"And Dr. Phillips, the veterinarian, reported that Thunder, your stallion, is fine. He just has a mild stomach upset that's not serious."

"Great. Let's call the senator first. Then schedule a meeting with Angela, Jeffrey, and Gordon for ten A.M. the day after tomorrow. Tell them I want updates on all their cases. See if you can arrange the TV interview for five o'clock tomorrow afternoon; at two I'm meeting with those Warner factory workers. What their boss expects from them harks back to slave labor."

"Try not to get beaten up, like the last time you were involved in management versus labor," Heather warned with a frown, and J.L. groaned, remembering the pain.

"I'll call my mother and the vet when I get a chance. Does that do it?"

"Yes, sir." Heather made notations on her steno pad, then started to leave, but J.L. waved his hand to stop her. "And don't stay late again tonight, Heather. I know you must have a life outside this law firm."

She blushed and fluttered her eyelashes at him. "I don't mind working late, Mr. Brett."

"Then I'll have to mind for you." He glanced at his watch, hardly believing it was nearly five o'clock. "Fifteen minutes and you're out of here."

"Will you be leaving, too? You need rest and relaxation as much as the rest of us."

J.L. shook his head no. "I want to go over my notes for that court case I'm trying tomorrow at eleven."

Heather sighed and shook her head as though he were impossible to reason with. "By the way, did you get out to the Lucky Dollar Mine?"

"Yes."

"Did you meet the woman who owns it?"

"Yes."

"What is she like?"

"She's...." J.L. searched for the right word by walking over to the floor-to-ceiling window where he stared out into the spring blue sky dotted with fluffy clouds scudding their way over bustling San Diego and a shimmering Pacific Ocean in the distance. What was the exact adjective he could use to describe a woman he couldn't stop thinking about?

"She's what, sir?"

"Different."

"How?"

"Oh, she's young, for one thing. I hadn't expected that. And argumentative. Spunky, actually. Smart. Pretty." He turned around and gazed at Heather who had a frown on her face. "She's not going to give up the money easily."

"Uh-oh."

"Anyway, that's for another day," J.L. closed the conversation and Heather, knowing his ways, left the room, closing the heavy door behind her.

With a dozen other things to sort through, J.L.'s thoughts, nevertheless, stayed with Lindsey Faraday. He had not expected so much resistance from her to his client's demands, but he was getting it. Lindsey's fierce belief in her father's innocence touched him, and warned him not to let personal admiration sway his professional duty. While he always enjoyed a challenge, he did not look forward to making someone suffer because of legal action taken against them, and it looked like that was exactly what was going to happen with Lindsey Faraday.

He spent the next three hours making phone calls, reviewing his notes for the next day's court case, which he expected would only last an hour at most, and further arranging his thoughts for his afternoon meeting with the factory workers. All the situations should not have taken long to complete, but he had trouble concentrating because a willowy blond kept drifting into his mind. This aggravated him no end but finally brought him to the decision that he would go back to the mine first thing the next day and fix the door he had torn from its frame. It was the least he could do.

five

After J.L. Brett left Lindsey's office, she worked for nearly two hours, going through the files of the Lucky Dollar Mine, searching for any paper that would show that her father had borrowed thirty thousand dollars back in 1985 from a woman named Francesca Owens. She found nothing, and was encouraged. Surely the whole situation was a mistake. All she had to do was prove it.

"You're working late, boss." She heard Santiago's familiar voice behind her and, turning, Lindsey saw her foreman standing just inside the door, frowning. Glancing at her watch, she was surprised to see that it was half past six. "It's been a long day, hasn't it?"

"Sure has. I checked out that jump hole on Level Nine like you told me to, and it won't be a problem to replace those timbers around it."

"I'm glad. There's always something, isn't there, Santiago, to keeping a mine safe?"

"That's the truth."

Lindsey went to her desk and gathered some papers into a manila folder that she then placed in the center drawer. She locked the drawer with a key.

"We're not in trouble, are we, boss?" Santiago surprised her by saying.

Lindsey stiffened, knowing he was referring to J.L. Brett's visit. While she was tempted to ask Santiago if he knew anything about a loan her father had received from a Francesca Owens, she decided against asking, knowing her father had done all his own bookkeeping and would not likely have

33

confided in the foreman. Also, if she could help it, she didn't want to involve Santiago in the problem or have him worrying whether or not he would have a job in a few months' time.

Even if he did know something about it, word of mouth would not help. She needed hard proof that the loan had been repaid *if*, as she still doubted, it had been made in the first place.

"Mr. Brett and I have some legal business that is tedious, Santiago," she answered him. "That's all." She smiled, hoping to reassure him and knowing he was concerned for her, just as he had been for many years.

In a way, Santiago Ramirez *was* the Lucky Dollar Mine. He had been a vital part of it for as long as she could remember, and before that even. When her father had purchased the mine, Santiago had offered to stay on and oversee it in return for reasonable pay and permission to continue to live, with his wife Maria and their five children, in a sturdy four-room cabin, made of weathered logs and at the end of the property, that they had occupied for many years, through several changes of ownership of the mine.

Since William Faraday had known little about gold mining, he had quickly agreed to the suggestion, and Santiago had become a part of their lives.

All through her childhood and teen years, Lindsey had followed the big man around, like a hungry puppy, asking countless questions, listening to his every word, amassing from him a formidable knowledge of gold and silver mining.

"You know you can always count on my help, don't you, boss?" Santiago asked her now.

Lindsey walked over to him and patted his bulky, hairy arm. "Of course I do."

"If you have any trouble with this Brett fella, you just let me know."

"Oh, I can handle J.L. Brett, Santiago."

He gave her a doubtful look.

"You and Larry, Pete, and Sanchez just keep the Lucky Dollar producing as healthfully as it is," she complimented him lavishly, "and maybe even find that elusive Mother Lode, then J.L. Brett won't be a problem."

They walked to where Santiago had propped the torn-off door against the wall. "I'll bring in a new one tomorrow," he promised. "Will the office be safe tonight without it?"

"There's not much to steal, Santiago. Besides, I don't lock it half the time anyway."

The foreman chuckled. "That's what I like about living in this area. People leave you alone."

"You're right."

They walked outside together. "Why don't you meet me on Level Two tomorrow, around nine o'clock," she said. "I didn't find the animal the men reported hearing there, but I want to check more closely for evidence of some kind."

"It could be that mountain lion."

"I know, but I sure hope not. Good night, Santiago."

Lindsey took a deep breath of fresh air and watched her foreman saunter down the path toward his humble home that stood a quarter of a mile away. What a charming place it was, surrounded entirely by purple and blue wildflowers, the path to its front porch bordered every spring with hundreds of yellow daffodils that had been lovingly planted by Maria, Santiago's wife.

How often she had gone there, Lindsey remembered, to play with Santiago's children who now were grown and living elsewhere, or to share a meal with this important family. But not tonight. Tonight she just wanted to get home, take a shower, relax with a good book, and hope she could quell the nagging feeling that was growing in her mind that today her life had taken a turn from which she might never recover, an unexpected turn caused by J.L. Brett and his client that was going to upset the life she had been content with for so many years.

Leaning against one of the posts that held up the slanted roof of the mine office and listening to the night silence that enveloped her, Lindsey contemplated the fact that she wasn't a millionaire by any means, but was able to support herself and her employees by doing something she loved—mining.

What would she do if she lost the Lucky Dollar? Teach? She could, for she had a degree in mining engineering. Work at some other mine? No, she only wanted to be at the one her father had owned, into which he had put the last years of his life.

Was that all she wanted? To work? Was it time for her to settle down and get married?

There was a man waiting for her to say yes—Lance Robards, a successful restaurateur from La Jolla with whom she had had six dates. She had met him while attending a birthday dinner for a friend of hers, held at one of his elite restaurants. He had seen her across the room, was intrigued (his word, not hers) by her, struck up a conversation with her when the celebration was over, invited her for a walk along the beach the next afternoon, took her to a concert in San Diego four nights later, and the dating began.

On their second date he said he was in love with her; on their third date he asked her to marry him, assuring her that he always made up his mind quickly and that they were perfect for each other.

But Lindsey was far too practical a woman to leap into marriage so quickly, and while she hadn't said yes to Lance's proposal, she hadn't said no either. She just wanted to get to know him better.

Lance was an attractive if not handsome man, with a short, stocky build and curly blond hair. Lindsey liked the green hue of his eyes but did not care for his pencil-thin moustache. He was easy to be with, good-natured, generous, romantic, and considerate. Those were his sterling qualities.

There were two areas, though, that concerned Lindsey and made her cautious. First of all, he could not fathom her love of the Lucky Dollar and, while he listened patiently when she talked about it, she wondered if he would want her to continue running it were they to be married.

Secondly, and even more troublesome, was Lance's disdain for Christianity. He impatiently claimed the church was out of touch with the real world, its precepts based on nothing more than archaic commandments, and that most supposed followers of Christ were hypocrites. He had been surprised when Lindsey boldly told him she had just given her heart to the Lord and considered the church a bastion against evil and a nurturing place of love and encouragement.

Lance, ever the diplomat, backtracked a little, and asked Lindsey to explain her beliefs to him, which she did, though she felt totally inadequate doing so since it was all so new to her. No one in her family had ever been a Christian, or even a nominal churchgoer, so Lindsey knew she was a baby Christian who had a long way to go to grow into spiritual maturity.

I wonder how J.L. Brett feels about God? she thought suddenly. *Is he a Christian?*

She meandered down to the small parking lot and got into her car, warning herself not to think of Mr. Brett in any other way than the threat that he was. He was not a new friend. He was not someone she should get to know personally. He had a job to do, and that job was to dispossess her of a great deal of money and perhaps even sell her beloved gold mine.

As Lindsey drove to her home in Majestic, population 1,300, with only ten streets running through its 150-year-old environs, she prayed to her Heavenly Father for guidance in her dilemma. Prayer was an act new to her, and thrilling. To think that she could actually speak to the God Who had created the universe, as intimately and often as she had spoken to her own father.

"Dear Lord, I don't know what tomorrow holds, or where the truth lies about this loan to my father, but You know. Lead me in the way I should go. Give me wisdom…and patience. In the name of Jesus, I pray."

The last part of her petition, for patience, meant she knew she would need to hold her sometimes volatile temper when it came to dealing with J.L. Brett. He was an exasperating man who was too sure of himself, too unbending.

After she had showered and put on a nightgown, a terrycloth robe, and old, floppy slippers, and had read ten pages of a book, Lindsey was ready for bed, but she could not stop thinking of the contemplative scrutiny of J.L. Brett, gazing at her earlier that day, making her aware of herself as a woman as she had not felt for a long time, even with Lance.

What had J.L. seen when he had looked at her so? Did he find her pretty or plain? Could he see beyond the minimal makeup to the soul that lay within her? Did he care what kind of person she was?

She hadn't looked her best today. Her hair had been wild and unstyled. She had been wearing dungarees and a work shirt. Even though J.L. Brett had been dressed casually, too, there was a sophistication about him in the way he expressed himself and moved that told her he was probably used to women who wore satin and lace and smelled like rose gardens.

Lindsey turned out the light and closed her eyes, willing herself to stop thinking about that varmint lawyer. The sooner this problem was settled and he was out of her life, the better she would like it.

six

J.L. knew he had given Lindsey three days to find some evidence to negate the claim that there was money owed his client. So, when he showed up at the office of the Lucky Dollar the very next morning, he told himself it was not to pressure her with the case, but merely to fix the door that he had ridiculously broken.

No one was around, so he put the broken door into the back of his truck to haul it away, and decided to just go ahead with the repair. He also noted that there was coffee brewing in a blue tin pot on the potbellied stove.

With tools in hand, he replaced the old splintered frame, attached new hinges and hung a thirty-two-inch-wide door that he had bought, and then started to paint it.

While he worked, he whistled, having a sense of comfort that the lady would be well-protected behind this rugged door. Protected from what or whom he did not know, but at least she wouldn't be vulnerable because he had lost his temper.

"How's it going?"

The deep voice came from behind him. Turning around, paint brush in hand, J.L. saw Santiago Ramirez, the mine foreman, watching him with a serious expression and his arms folded over his wide chest. His old blue jeans were held up with green suspenders and the sleeves of his lightweight woolen black shirt were rolled up to the elbow. There was a chill in the morning air, from the altitude, but J.L. found it refreshing even though he was in short sleeves.

"Good morning," he greeted Santiago cheerfully. Motioning toward the door he said, "I thought I'd better fix it since

I'm the one who destroyed it."

"Nice door."

"Yep. Should last a few years."

J.L. put the finishing stroke of dusky brown latex enamel paint on the door, then squatted beside a jar of soapy water and began cleaning his brush in it.

"I'll have one of the men put the knob and lock on later," Santiago offered.

"I'll do it myself, if you don't mind," J.L. countered. "I'm sure your guys have other things to do." .

Santiago shrugged and said, "Okay."

J.L. wiped his hands on a piece of rag and asked, "Is Miss Faraday coming in today?"

Santiago looked at his watch. "Should be here by eight. It's ten to now."

"Great. Is there any chance I can get a cup of that coffee brewing on the stove?"

"Sure."

Santiago went into the office, returning moments later with a paper cup filled to the brim. He handed the steaming liquid to J.L. who smelled it coming and took a deep draft, finding it to be just what he had expected: miner's brew, strong enough to walk by itself. Knowing the foreman was waiting for him to spit out the awful stuff, he exclaimed, "Now that's what I call a cup of coffee. Thanks, Santiago."

The foreman frowned. "If you want more, just help yourself."

"Will do."

J.L. swished the brush in the soapy water again and said casually, "You're a man of many talents, Santiago. Does Miss Faraday pay you what you're worth?"

He could tell from the way Santiago's eyes narrowed almost shut that the man was wary and might not answer at all.

"Why do you want to know?" Santiago grunted.

"Because I help employees get fair treatment from their employers. If you're not paid enough, or working conditions are poor—"

Santiago jutted his chin out in a defiant gesture. "Miss Lindsey is good to us."

"Is she?"

J.L. captured Santiago's gaze with his own, wondering how much of the man's declaration was truth and how much was loyalty. He took another gulp of coffee. "Are your wages comparable to what other mine workers make, Santiago? Do you have health benefits and a pension plan?"

"You should be asking me those questions," a feminine voice interrupted, and J.L. turned to see Lindsey Faraday in the doorway, holding a briefcase with both hands, her right side just inches from the newly painted door. From the frown that creased her narrow forehead, she either had not had her first cup of coffee of the day, or she was not happy to see him.

J.L. jumped forward, grabbed both her arms, and pulled her away from the door.

"What are you doing?" she yelped, her gleaming blue eyes sparking as she fell into his arms, her hands clutching him for support.

"Keeping you clean."

J.L. turned her around, still holding her waist, and pointed toward the door. "Fresh paint."

"Oh."

Lindsey regained her balance and stepped away from J.L., looked at the door and at the paint stains on his Levi's and hands, and at Santiago, who shrugged his shoulders and said, "He was here when I got here, boss."

She looked back at J.L. "Penance, Mr. Brett?"

He nodded without a word. She was doing it again, taking his breath away with her long, straight hair flowing down to her shoulders and her feisty blue eyes matching the shade of the cotton blouse she wore. Her dungarees were black today, as were her low-heeled boots, and her mood.

Lindsey walked back to the door, inspected it, and then turned and gave J.L. a smile of three on a scale of one to ten. "You've gone to a lot of trouble for us, Mr. Brett, and I thank you for it, especially since I am partially to blame for the door being torn from its hinges."

"You are?"

"You wouldn't have pulled it off if you hadn't been angry with me," she surprised him by saying. "Isn't that true?"

J.L. nodded cautiously. "But you didn't make me lose my temper. I did that all by myself."

Lindsey acknowledged the truth of that statement by nodding her head, and then her smile disappeared and was replaced by an annoyed expression.

"While I thank you for the door, Mr. Brett, I do not thank you for trying to stir up trouble with my employees. Why were you asking Santiago about how I treat my people?"

"I'll explain over breakfast."

Lindsey shook her head. "I don't eat breakfast."

"That's a bad habit. It's important to get the metabolism started in the morning."

"I work better on an empty stomach."

"The experts don't agree."

"The experts don't have my stomach."

As though an imaginary line had been drawn between them, they each stood their ground, and Santiago looked from one to the other before shaking his head in puzzlement and then leaving the office.

"Now, about breakfast," J.L. began again.

"No," Lindsey said firmly, and meant it.

"It's not a personal invitation," he assured her, trying to fool himself. "I have to wait till the paint dries before I can put in the door handle and lock."

"One of my men will do that."

One of her men, J.L. thought. *One of her men. She is surrounded by men.* That bothered him.

"Santiago offered the same help," he said, "but I told him I'd rather complete the job myself."

Lindsey walked over to the desk and set her briefcase down in the middle of it with a decided thud, then began extricating papers and folders, trying to calm her frustration.

She didn't want him here, reminding her of the loan. Didn't want him asking questions of her employees, insinuating she wasn't fair to them. *Is that how he gets business, by dredging up trouble?* she wondered.

"I'm sure you have far more important things to do, Mr. Brett, than play handyman," she said flatly.

J.L. looked at his watch. "Not till later this morning when I have to be in court."

"Humph," Lindsey grunted, taking some of the papers over to a nearby file cabinet that had more than its share of dents in the sides. She opened the top drawer. "Evicting a little old lady from her family home?" she quipped.

J.L. chuckled. "Fighting for proper living conditions for migrant workers. Bigger cabins. Better facilities."

"Bravo," she said.

Lindsey was shocked at herself. She wasn't a mean person, but she was being mean to him and just couldn't help it. Everything about him irritated her. Well, almost everything. He was wearing a red short-sleeved shirt and she had noticed the muscles along his forearms tense and ripple as he had grabbed for her and held her, and the heavy forest of dark hair on his arms that she had felt beneath her fingers had only reminded her of how masculine he was.

She began plopping papers into any old file she came to, not even realizing what she was doing.

"All of that sounds far more important than fixing a broken

door," she said, feeling a little short of breath.

"More important perhaps, but not more enjoyable." His husky voice sent shivers down Lindsey's spine and she didn't dare look at him after that remark. She didn't have to. She remembered the shine of his hair and its smell of recent shampoo, both of which she had noticed when she had been in his arms.

His shoulders were broad.

His hands strong.

His waist trim.

Lindsey slammed the file cabinet shut and J.L. jumped.

"Something wrong?" he inquired, figuring, *Here it comes, the order to get off her property, the call for Santiago to draw and quarter me, the whistle for the marauding mountain lion to come and have me for breakfast.*

"Not one thing."

"Ready for breakfast, then?" He was, above all, a persistent man and an optimist.

"Not today, thanks." Lindsey strode over to him. "Let me help you with your tools. I'm sure you must be going."

J.L. got the message and decided not to annoy her any more than she already was, but he sure would have to underline "temperamental" on his list of her faults.

He leaned down to pick up a screwdriver at exactly the same moment Lindsey reached for the same one. They bumped, straightened quickly, and then Lindsey screamed. Her hair was caught in one of the metal buttons of his western shirt.

Lindsey's head was practically on his chest, and she was so off balance that J.L. had to put his arms around her to hold her up. Their bodies pressed together and drew apart as she fought desperately to get away.

"Do something!" she ordered.

"I will if you stop squirming," he promised, trying to hold her steady with one arm while his bulky fingers worked through the silky texture of her hair to untangle her from his shirt button. "Stop fidgeting."

"I can't help it, you're hurting me."

"Not intentionally."

"I'll bet. Ow!"

Lindsey's scalp felt like it was being jerked from her head, and her hands clutched J.L.'s arms, feeling the strength that supported her helplessness, while her ears, so near his chest, heard the rapid beating of his heart and knew it matched her own.

She made the mistake of turning up her head just as J.L. looked down. His dark eyes captured hers and their gazes held. Her lips opened and their faces moved slowly toward each other.

"Hold very still," J.L. whispered.

Lindsey obeyed as his arm around her waist pulled her firmly against him and the fingers of his other hand worked the hair loose that was caught, but stayed long enough to meander through the thickness of it. His face touched its softness and an almost inaudible groan escaped him.

Lindsey closed her eyes and felt his lips brush the curve of her cheek. His mouth was soft and moist and her skin tingled and the sensation raced through her like a laser beam. His lips touched the corner of her mouth and Lindsey feared her knees would give way. Her fingers gripped his supporting arm, and she turned into his kiss that was gentle and fleeting and left her wanting more.

seven

The kiss was light and over in a second, but J.L. knew he had wanted it to happen. And when he looked deeply into Lindsey's eyes, he saw in those mesmerizing blue diamonds the same acceptance of this crazy moment in time that they had been given.

Tiny wheat-colored lashes swept around the bottom of her eyes, and long, gently curved lashes defined their brilliance as she gazed up at him in silent surprise.

Without thinking, he brushed the back of his fingers across Lindsey's cheek, and she did not recoil, but he wondered what she would do if he tried to kiss her again.

Deciding he would be wise to retreat with his limbs intact, he straightened up, still holding her near, their eyes never leaving each other's. Hands on her waist, he held her lightly until her gaze lowered, in embarrassment, and the moment was broken.

Lindsey struggled to regain her composure, caught off guard by what had happened, confused that so simple a kiss could tumble her emotions and make her moan with pleasure. Or had that sound come from him?

Now safely on her feet and with her hair free, rational thought returned to her mind, but her cheeks were still warm from his touch and she realized: *I just kissed the enemy.* Her heart skipped a beat. *How could I have done that?*

J.L. cleared his throat. "I think it's time for breakfast."

"No." Lindsey stepped away from his hands.

"Yes." J.L. firmly took her elbow and, despite feeble resistance, ushered her through the new door and down the path to his truck.

46

Snooks and Bones, two scraggly dogs of indiscriminate parentage, tagged after them, cavorting at their feet, hoping for a pat on the head and a kind word. But neither Lindsey nor J.L. had room in their thoughts for anyone but each other, and they were both thinking the same thing: *That kiss should never have happened. Why did I enjoy it so much?*

When they reached the gravel parking lot and a burgundy, half-ton, 4x4 pickup with oversized tires and gray-and-burgundy striping down the sides, Lindsey considered the truck that was not all that clean, and observed dryly, "I assume you're a successful lawyer, Mr. Brett, but you dress like a cowboy and drive a truck. Why?" She suspected there was another side of him that wore a tuxedo and drove a red Porsche.

J.L. laughed softly and opened the door for her. "Don't tell me you're more impressed by a man's possessions than by the man himself?"

Lindsey gulped. "Certainly not."

"Then that was just an idle comment and not meant to put me down for my choice of clothes or vehicle?"

Those diamond eyes that he had eulogized rounded into twin circles of fire. "I wasn't doing that."

"I didn't think so."

He watched her get in, closed her door, then strode around to the driver's side and slid behind the wheel, putting the key in the ignition. Turning to her he said, "Even though you're wearing dungarees instead of a frilly dress, I still think you're beautiful."

"What?"

His eyes twinkled. "And though you work in a dirty mine and let your hair hang loose and wild, that's no sign you're less feminine than any other woman."

Lindsey's cheeks flamed with indignation. "I don't really care whether or not you like my wardrobe and hair style." She flung the words at him, and her hand reached for the door handle.

J.L. chuckled and brought the engine to life, driving off

before she could escape. "Just making an observation, Miss Faraday, not a judgment."

Lindsey sat tensely in the seat, staring straight ahead, while J.L. expertly maneuvered the pickup onto the narrow country road and headed toward Majestic, the nearest town, about two miles away. She said not a word but once did surreptitiously glance over at him and noticed how strong his hands were as they gripped the leather-covered steering wheel, how in control he was of this powerful machine...and, at the moment, of her.

Suppressing a deep sigh, she returned her gaze forward and knew she was in trouble.

Without being guided, J.L. took her to her favorite restaurant, a cheerful and homey place with sunlight dancing through spotless windows where blue-and-white gingham curtains carried their colors through to the blue wooden benches and white wicker plant holders from which tumbled healthy green philodendron.

The smell of the place was of freshly baked cinnamon rolls and glazed donuts the size of pancakes, and the crowd of happily chattering adults and giggly teenagers spoke well of its reputation for fine food.

Lindsey perused the menu and battled her self-will that yearned for one of the cinnamon rolls dripping with white icing, instead of choosing something sensible and healthy. Whenever she was upset, she usually ate something gooey, rich, and fattening, and right now, sitting across from J.L. Brett, the enemy, whose kiss had, nevertheless, been devastating, and who had told her she was beautiful despite the fact that she wore dungarees and worked in a dirty mine, she felt the temptation to abandon common sense.

With amazement she listened to J.L. order "a Denver omelet, double order of bacon, hash browns, a blueberry muffin, and the largest orange juice you have." *How can he have such a gorgeous physique when he eats all that gook?* she wondered, knowing she would be gaining two pounds just watching him eat it all.

"I'll take a bran muffin and tomato juice," she said, overcoming temptation, and the waitress, a young girl of about nineteen, her dark hair in a curly ponytail, wrote down the orders while gazing in admiration at J.L., as though he were Tom Cruise and Rhett Butler in the same body.

"Coffee?" she asked with an eager child's voice.

"Yes, please," J.L. answered with a winning smile, and the girl fell over her feet scurrying away, without asking Lindsey if she wanted any.

She soon returned with a full pot of steaming coffee that looked too heavy for her to carry. When J.L. gave her another million-dollar smile that brought out the two dimples in his cheeks, her body went limp, she gave him a goo-goo smile, giggled nervously, and poured the coffee way too fast, over the cup and saucer, onto the table.

J.L. and Lindsey both gasped, and the waitress did, too, and grabbed the nearest cloth napkin and frantically tried to mop up the scalding liquid. But when her pencil fell into the cup, and she anxiously tried to retrieve it, that's when the cup tipped over, sending the scalding liquid running off the table and onto J.L.'s lap.

As the waitress reached to clean up the table, she tipped the pot in her hand, and more coffee plummeted out.

Lindsey and J.L. both scrambled out of the booth. Lindsey missed disaster, but J.L. didn't. Most of the mess went on him, staining his jeans even more.

"Oh, no," the girl screamed and dashed away to get a towel, which she brought quickly and thrust at J.L., who pressed it carefully against the soaked material. A busboy came to work on the table.

"We'll move," Lindsey told the distraught girl with a straight face. She didn't want to laugh. She tried very hard not to laugh, but a snicker escaped from behind her hand and J.L. glared at her as they seated themselves in another booth.

"I don't see what is funny here," he said.

Immediately Lindsey forced an innocent expression to her face. "Neither do I," she fibbed, and told the waitress, "Could you bring the gentleman a clean towel, please." She turned to J.L. "If you put water on those jeans right away, they'll be okay." She paused. "Was it hot?"

He looked at her as though she were daft. "Of course it was hot. Coffee is always hot. That's what the swirls of steam mean."

"I see."

The girl brought the towel, J.L. excused himself to go to the washroom, and Lindsey chuckled to herself over the mishap. How fortunate J.L. was wearing blue jeans rather than dress slacks, she thought as she watched the unhappy girl explaining to her supervisor what had happened. Lindsey felt sorry for her, knowing that waiting on such a handsome male as J.L. Brett had unnerved her.

When he returned to the table, Lindsey asked, "Everything all right?"

"Yes," he said sharply. "Is this the only restaurant in town?"

"No, but it is one of the best."

She nodded toward the waitress who was sniffling into a tissue, and J.L. understood her silent suggestion and immediately got up and went over to the girl, gently touching her arm while assuring her that no harm had been done.

Lindsey felt the power of his charisma, and the sincerity of his gentlemanly gesture, even from a distance and, when the waitress gave him a beatific smile of adoration, she was not surprised.

He probably is a nice guy, she thought for an instant, but then changed her mind. *No, he's trouble.*

J.L. returned and slid into the booth. "This is her first day," he reported with a look of sympathy. "I asked for coffee for you." He grinned. "You did want some, didn't you?"

"Yes, Mr. Brett," Lindsey answered tentatively, and kept her eyes glued to the young waitress who, this time, did a perfect job pouring it into Lindsey's cup.

"Thanks, Tina," J.L. said, and the girl fluttered her eyes,

blushed, and managed to move on to the next table without having an accident.

"On a first-name basis already?" Lindsey quipped after the girl had gone.

J.L. gave her a long look. "That's more than I can say for us, isn't it?"

Lindsey took a long sip of the very good coffee before murmuring, "I don't see any reason for us to get more familiar."

J.L. captured her gaze. "Don't you?"

There was an awkward silence in which both of them wondered what would really happen if they forgot they were on opposite sides of a legal case.

"So," J.L. finally broke the contemplation, "how many employees do you have?"

Lindsey eyed him suspiciously. "Why do you want to know?"

"Just curious."

Lindsey shook her head in disbelief. "This has to do with what you were asking Santiago about his wages and benefits?"

J.L. returned her direct gaze. "In a way, I suppose."

"Ask another question. I don't want to argue over a meal. It's bad for the stomach."

"Who says we're going to argue?"

"A good guess since we don't seem to be able to say two words to each other without disagreeing."

"I don't have that problem with anyone else."

"Neither do I."

They both drank from their cups.

J.L. took a deep breath and let it out. "Does it get very hot up at the mine in the summer?"

Lindsey's eyes narrowed. "Yes, it does."

"Do you think it will rain today?" J.L. picked up his fork as their meals arrived.

"No, it will not rain," Lindsey returned sharply, looking at her paltry muffin, wishing it were a gooey cinnamon roll, "and why are my employees of interest to you?" Better to understand the enemy than ignore him, she now decided.

J.L. took a man-sized bite of omelet, chewed it thoroughly, and swallowed it, never taking his eyes off Lindsey, then answered, "Because a lot of workers don't make adequate salaries or receive the benefits they should."

"Were you thinking about representing my employees against me, Mr. Brett?" She tore off a chunk of her bran muffin and popped it into her mouth, without even adding soft butter.

"Do they need representing?"

"Certainly not." She glared at him. "The Lucky Dollar isn't a wealthy mine, but I do everything I can to provide for the four people who work for it." Her voice was steady, her gaze sure, because she knew she was a good employer.

"So, you have health coverage?"

"Yes, of course."

"And a pension plan?"

Lindsey hesitated. "I will have. Some day soon. That costs a lot of money."

"Every worker needs a secure future, especially if he's not highly paid. Social Security isn't enough to live on for most people."

Lindsey knew the truth of that, but she was miffed that J.L. was pointing it out to her. "I want my employees to be fully protected. Right now, though, every dollar is earmarked for salaries or mine operation." And a pitiful amount in savings, she could have added, knowing J.L. Brett would be shocked to learn what that was and also what a tiny salary she took for herself.

"Let's get back to enjoying our breakfast," J.L. suggested. "I don't want to upset you."

Lindsey's eyes blazed. "How can I not be upset when you're trying to take a great amount of money from my company *and* stir up trouble with my employees?"

"Now wait a minute, that's not fair," J.L. complained, leaning forward and reaching for Lindsey's hand. She quickly withdrew, accidentally knocking over his coffee, which knew where to go and ran directly off the table, onto his lap.

eight

"Not again," J.L. howled; people turned to look, Tina hurried over with another towel, the busboy shuffled over to attend to the table, and this time Lindsey laughed out loud.

"Let's get out of here," J.L. growled, whipping some bills out of his wallet and thrusting them into Tina's hands. "Here you go, kid." He held the door open for Lindsey, but she tugged at his arm.

"Don't you want to...?" She glanced demurely downward.

J.L. assessed the latest damage. "Oh...yeah," and he strode off, again, to the washroom.

"He'll be okay, Tina," Lindsey assured the girl, who looked like she had lost her last friend.

"He called me a kid," she blubbered, burst into tears, and ran out the front door.

J.L. came back, a watermark all too discernible on his jeans. "I'm starving. Where else can we eat?"

They had an uneventful breakfast at the Apple Orchard coffee shop, talking only of national news and the latest books they had read. With a little effort, they managed not to get into another argument and they were both glad, because when they finished and went outside, it was one of those balmy, sunny days when one is glad to be alive and wants only to be happy.

On the way to the truck, the song of tiny birds chirping madly in nearby trees caught their attention and J.L. said, "Maybe we should play hooky and enjoy this day."

Lindsey quickened her step instead of slowing it.

"Playing hooky is for children, Mr. Brett. Besides, you have to be in court, and I have a Full Reconveyance to find."

The words were a little sharper than she had intended but true enough, and only her finding some proof that the loan had either been paid, or had never been made in the first place, would get J.L. Brett and his client out of her life. And that's what she wanted, wasn't it?

"How about a short walk, then?" he suggested. Lindsey resisted but finally allowed him to talk her into a few more minutes with him.

They strolled past the Majestic Hotel built in 1897, and went into an antique shop when J.L. saw a piece of Victorian cranberry glass he thought his mother would like. At the cider mill, he insisted on checking out the many shelves of specialty candies, nuts, syrups, jams, and jellies.

"In the winter, the locals sit around the parlor stove and sip hot apple cider and converse over the events of the day," Lindsey told him after he had bought her a bag of licorice buttons.

"That's great."

"Do you really think so?"

"Yeah, I do."

"Things move slowly in Majestic compared with San Diego," she admitted.

"Nothin' wrong with that. There's a time for fast and a time for slow." His gaze drifted over her hair and settled on her lips.

"It's a quiet town, a quaint place," she said, starting their walk again, which was better than standing still and gazing into his hypnotic eyes. "Streets A, B, C, and D run parallel to Main, and First through Fifth cross east and west. One can walk through it in half an hour, if you don't stop to look in the pretty shops or to have a piece of warm apple pie."

"Majestic is well-known for its apple orchards, isn't it?"

"Yes, and for its history that really began when gold was discovered in 1869. The earth around here has given up thirteen million dollars worth over the years."

J.L. whistled through his teeth. "I guess it was a real boom town once."

"Yes, indeed, with six hotels, four general stores, a dozen saloons, two stage lines to San Diego, and thousands of miners, all with a dreams of hitting it big."

"I like the way it's evolved."

"You do?"

"Yes. It has personality. This morning I drove around a little before coming to the mine."

Lindsey was stunned. She remembered Lance thinking the town was horrible. "What do people do for entertainment?" he had asked, and when Lindsey had asked if he would ever open a restaurant there, he had gaped at her as though she were mad and responded, "Not in a thousand years."

Then he had gone on to say the hotel was too small for his taste, the cider mill and antique shops looked depressingly unprofitable, and not even sampling the biggest slice of apple pie in Majestic, at the Green and Yellow Cafe on Second Street, had impressed him. "Way too much sugar," he had groaned, and Lindsey had sighed and felt a little miffed at his lack of appreciation for her town.

But J.L. liked Majestic, and this inched him one notch higher on Lindsey's approval ladder.

"Do you live in town?" he asked.

"On the outskirts, but it's not far from here."

"Do you want to show me?"

Lindsey shook her head no. "I have to get back to the mine. This is way later than I normally start work." Besides, showing her home to J.L. Brett was too personal a gesture for her. It wasn't as though they were starting to date and would ever mean anything to each other.

"Actually, I have to get back, too," he said, "but I'll put the knob and lock on your door first."

"Santiago can do that," Lindsey suggested.

"Santiago didn't break the door."

They were at the truck and J.L. started to open the passenger door for Lindsey just as she reached for it herself. Their hands collided on the hard, hot metal of the handle, and Lindsey froze.

"Thank you for having breakfast with me," J.L. said softly in her ear, his body too near, his scent triggering a response in Lindsey that unnerved her. It would be so easy to turn, just one slight turn, and she would be in his arms, and he would kiss her again, she knew he would, and a part of her would relish it.

She yearned to be a woman desired and cherished, the awareness welling up from deep inside her where it had been held down by years of hard work, determination to fulfill her father's dream, and the lack of any man to ignite her passions. Would there be passion with J.L.?

Stepping back abruptly, full length against his muscled chest and legs, Lindsey jerked the door open and slid onto the seat. What was the matter with her, having romantic fantasies about this man who was here to destroy her life?

She stared straight ahead when he closed the door, then walked around the front of the truck and got in beside her. She stared, and tried not to let the sound of her breathing be heard.

He sat there, leaning his arms on the steering wheel, and she knew he was battling strange feelings, too, and the silence and inactivity stirred Lindsey's impatience as she tried to control a crazy urge to fling herself into his arms.

Thankfully, just as her nerves reached the end of their tether, he started the truck and drove to C Street where he turned right, onto the narrow road that led to the mine.

"I'll come out and see you in few days, Lindsey, to get things straightened out."

"Please call for an appointment first," she answered stiffly, trying to put him off. She had to keep him at arm's length or she would make a mistake and give him her heart—a mistake she knew she would regret.

She was unprepared for the soft chuckle that resonated through the cab of the truck. "No, darlin', I'll just show up," he said, "because if I call, you'll find some way to electrocute me through the phone lines."

"What an interesting thought."

"Why are you so anxious to not like me?"

Lindsey couldn't help sighing. "The circumstances that have brought us together make it impossible for me to like you and your greedy client."

A frown moved his heavy eyebrows down to a vee. "You shouldn't judge people you don't know. My client is an honorable person, and I'm really a nice guy. In fact, I love children, and haven't kicked a dog since I was ten and was being bitten by one."

"How touching."

"So, can we be friends?"

"I don't see how."

"Certainly not enemies."

There was a twinkle in his eyes that Lindsey couldn't believe. Why wasn't he put off by her standoffish attitude? "Adversaries is a better word," she said. "That's all we can be to each other."

J.L. chuckled and said, "How wrong you are, Miss Faraday," and he continued driving down the road toward the mine, the mine that had brought them together, and the mine that would very likely keep them apart.

nine

For five days J.L. didn't come back to the mine. He didn't even phone for five days, and Lindsey wondered why. Was he simply giving her more time to find a way to defend her position, or had he told her she was beautiful, taken her to breakfast, and been fun to be with just so he could find ammunition to enable him to win his case for his client?

She didn't want to think that. She was not a cynical person by temperament, but she was fighting for her life now, her dream, and her father's. *I won't allow myself to be attracted to him,* she decided, *and I won't spend any more time with him than what is absolutely necessary.*

The phone rang.

"Lindsey? Hello. This is J.L. How are you?"

"Hi." The sound of his voice, so deep and rich, familiarly speaking her first name, carried through the receiver and washed over Lindsey like warm milk, soothing her anxious feelings, toying with her decision to have as little to do with him as possible. It was not going to be easy to keep this man at bay, but she knew she had to if she was going to win against him.

"I'd like to see you this afternoon," he said. "Would two o'clock be all right?"

Lindsey didn't hesitate. "I'm afraid not. I have tourists going through the mine." She sounded stiff when she wanted to sound self-confident, as though hearing from him meant nothing at all, and seeing him was of no importance to her.

"How long will the tour last?"

"An hour or so."

"Fine. I can be there at three-thirty or four."

Lindsey squelched a sigh. The man was tracking his prey and

not about to give up. "That won't work, either," she told him.

"Oh?"

"I…I have a meeting with my attorney." That was the truth. She had a friend who was a lawyer, and the day after her breakfast with J.L., she had called him and asked him for advice and also to check on the track record of one J.L. Brett of San Diego. "I'm sorry, but it really will be impossible to see you this afternoon."

"This evening, then. You just name the time."

"No. This evening is not good, either."

There was no immediate response from him and Lindsey wondered what he was thinking, what he was planning.

Finally he said coldly, "Lindsey, I'm not asking for a date. This is a business meeting, and one we have to have. It's in your best interest as well as mine."

"That's highly questionable," she retorted, the steel in his voice infuriating her. She didn't like being told what to do, even though she knew he was right: they had to see each other for legal reasons, if for no other. "Why don't you just drop me a letter, and I'll answer with one?"

"Fine." The word was sharp.

She started to hang up, breathing a sigh of relief. She had done it—fended him off, for now. Hopefully her lawyer friend, John Gregory, would have a brilliant idea on how she could defeat this self-assured adversary. There had to be a way she could keep her mine. Then she heard J.L. call her name, "Lindsey?"

"Yes?" She quickly brought the receiver back to her ear.

"Thanks for not electrocuting me through the phone." He laughed softly. "Goodbye, beautiful."

He hung up, and Lindsey stared at the phone for more than a minute before putting it down. He had called her beautiful again, and he shouldn't have, for she was sure she was not at all beautiful to a sophisticated man like him.

❧

For the next hour Lindsey went through, again, every file that might possibly have anything to do with a loan made years ago. But she found nothing and was therefore frustrated and not in the best of moods when it came time to take the small group of tourists through the mine.

She wished she didn't have to conduct tours in order to help pay the bills. The Lucky Dollar gave up enough minerals each month to support her and her employees, but mining expenses were astronomical and the money went out as fast as it came in. She needed tourist revenue, so she met the strangers with as good a smile as she could muster, determined to do her very best to bring to them the excitement and history of this fascinating place.

When she led the group into the Lucky Dollar, a tingle of anticipation raced up her back and over her shoulders as the rocky, sedimentary walls surrounded her. Even though she had entered this tunnel a thousand times before, the thrill she now experienced was as deep and wondrous as it had been that very first time she had been brought there, at the age of eight, by her father.

On that unforgettable day she had clung tightly to his smooth, cool hand as he had led her along, only a little afraid when the light from the outside world faded and the unusual darkness that comes from being underground began to engulf them. She knew she was safe as long as she was with her daddy, holding his hand.

But he wasn't there anymore, and today, as she faced seven eager people staring expectantly at her when she stopped them a ways inside the mine, she knew she was in the hands of another Father, a Father she could not touch or hear but Whom she knew loved her and Who had promised never to leave or forsake her. He would be her Father forever, for eternity, but He was also interested in every day of her life, every moment. He was there right now, His Spirit within her, caring, able to guide her. "Thank You, Father," she whispered in the muted darkness of the mine and in that moment, felt His presence, and His peace.

"Ladies and gentlemen," she addressed the three married couples and the small fidgety boy, tugging at his mother's slacks and whining for a piece of gum, "welcome to the Lucky Dollar.

"This is an actual working mine. Gold, silver, and platinum are being extracted from it today, as they have been since the year 1870 when the mine was discovered and registered."

The little boy got his gum and threw the wrapper down on the ground. Without a frown, Lindsey picked it up and stuffed it into the back pocket of her jeans.

"Let me remind you to stay close to me as we move along," she instructed, and then was interrupted by the sound of someone running toward them. Everyone turned around and saw a tall, ruggedly built man approaching. It was J.L.

He was dressed in a business suit, white shirt, and tie, and looked more ready for a day in the office than a tour of a dusty mine. His hair, tousled over his forehead, softened the sharp planes of his face, as did the triumphant smile that, to Lindsey, was actually a smirk.

He held out a ticket to her. "A man in the office said you'd just started the tour, and that I could still make it."

He wasn't breathing hard after his run, and he stared right at her with intense brown eyes and an innocent expression. Lindsey wondered how she could trigger a cave-in that would fall only on him and not anyone else. "I hope I haven't missed anything," he said.

Without returning his smile, Lindsey took the ticket from him and remarked, "No, we've just started, but I was telling the folks to stay close to me—"

"No problem."

"And do exactly as I say."

"Yes, ma'am." His eyes were twinkling.

Lindsey looked at the rest of the group, because it was infinitely easier than looking at J.L. Brett, who was making her dander rise because he had blatantly come here when she had expressly told him not to. Obviously, he was a man who did not take orders well.

"Please do not wander down any of the side tunnels to explore on your own," she told them all. "There are eleven levels to this mine, and numerous holes that drop hundreds of feet into a black abyss. There is danger here, but respect that danger and you won't get lost or hurt."

"Or abandoned?" J.L. quipped, and the others made nervous sounds and glanced at the walls that entombed them, while Lindsey hurriedly said, "Certainly not," although it was an intriguing idea if it meant getting him out of her sight.

Lindsey began to walk and J.L. fell in beside her, much to her dismay. "It will be dark in many places where we don't have electricity," she warned, "so walk carefully. We have left it this way so you can get the true feeling of a mine in its natural setting."

As the natural light diminished, Lindsey turned on a heavy-duty flashlight and used it to guide them along the dirt path ahead.

In a few seconds they reached their first stop, where Lindsey flipped on a single light bulb that illuminated the surroundings. The tunnel here was fairly wide and well over six feet in height, and she noticed that the top of J.L.'s head was only inches from the rocky ceiling. And his tightly muscled body was only inches from her own.

She took a step to her right and directed her flashlight along the rocky wall. "Geologists tell us that at the dawn of creation this area of southern California was a seabed, and that enormous pressure deep within the earth finally heaved it upward to form this mountain range."

She could feel J.L.'s eyes surveying her.

"When this occurred, the seabed tilted from the horizontal to approximately eighty-two degrees, and cracks and crevices occurred in the rock. Hot gasses, solutions, and molten rock surged up from down below and filled those crevices, and because it was virgin rock it was heavily mineralized. When it cooled, it formed the quartz veins in which the gold, silver, and platinum lie."

She was unprepared when one of J.L.'s strong hands surrounded hers that held the flashlight and directed it to another part of the wall.

"Is that a quartz vein?" he asked in resonant tones that reminded her of thick, dark, hot fudge sliding over a mound of rapidly warming vanilla ice cream. She was the ice cream, trying to stay firm, but knowing she would soon melt if she stayed too close to him.

She quickly withdrew her hand from his grasp.

"Yes, it is a vein," she told him and the others in a voice that quivered, to her consternation. "It runs from here clear through the mountain and widens out to between two and three feet on the other end. Notice the color. That means there's a mineral there. Every mineral has its own color, and a miner will say that quartz with color has a 'kindly' look, while one without color is 'hungry.' This one is kindly."

Lindsey stepped aside so the others in her group could move closer to see what she was highlighting with her flashlight. A tourist asked a question, which she answered with authority, and J.L. asked, with undisguised admiration in his voice, "Do you really know this much about mining, or have you memorized a speech?"

Lindsey thought of all the years she had spent getting a college degree and exploring these tunnels with her foreman, Santiago Ramirez, and other miners, learning every square inch of the miles and miles of it.

"Let's just say I have a retentive memory," she said, moving away from J.L., for he made her uncomfortable. She was used to being around men, had been surrounded by them most of her life, but none had made her feel the way he did, strangely aware of her own femininity, or lack of it. Not even Lance made her respond so.

Self-consciously, she tucked behind her ear an errant strand of pale blond hair that had fallen out of her ponytail and then she started to move on. But J.L.'s arm shot out in front of her, blocking her way, the palm of his hand flat against the wall.

"I think there's more to your knowledge of gold mining than a good memory," he said. "Tell us, please, how a young and charming woman like yourself knows so much about it."

"Yes, tell us," several of the tourists echoed his request.

He was too close to her. In the semidark, without even touching her, J.L. assaulted Lindsey's senses and she grappled with the horrible truth that he was unbelievably appealing to her.

"I have a degree in mining engineering," she finally said, not at all at ease talking about herself, "from the Colorado School of Mines."

"A prestigious school," J.L. said. "What subjects did you have to take?"

"Physics, chemistry, mathematics, civil, mechanical, and electrical engineering."

He whistled. "Impressive. Four-point-0 grade/point average, I'll bet."

"Three-point-eight, actually."

"Slipped up somewhere, hmm?"

"Let's just get on with the tour, Mr. Brett."

"Of course." He lowered his arm. "Now that I know that you know what you're talking about, I'll pay more attention."

To what? Lindsey wondered. *Me or the mine?*

"Miss," a heavyset woman in a snug-fitting pantsuit addressed her, "how do you get the gold out of these rocks?"

"I'll explain it at our next stop," Lindsey said to the woman, which she did, reciting by rote the facts she had given hundreds of times before, that miners drilled alongside the quartz vein where possible, in the softer sedimentary rock, enabling explosives to be used to bring out the quartz, also known as ore.

"When we get outside, to the stamp mill," she promised the attentive woman, "I'll show you how the gold is extracted from the ore."

But that's forty-five minutes from now, Lindsey realized, as her stomach tightened. Her palms were already wet and her breathing shallower than usual. Her head was even throbbing a little. Was she coming down with the flu?

ten

The tour continued along narrow tunnels, down stairs and ladders, around corners, descending gradual paths leading further and further into the bowels of the earth, and always, Lindsey was aware of the presence of J.L. Brett.

Only when the group emerged into daylight some time later did Lindsey feel more at ease, the bright, warming sunshine a relief from the intimate darkness of the tunnels and the intimate closeness of J.L. Brett.

He was standing away from her now, talking with one of the other men, and she began to breathe normally as she showed the people the unique Cornish stamp mill, not in use at the moment, and the mortar box in it, in which the ore from the mine was placed, after having been precrushed in a jaw crusher.

"The mill has two stamps, each weighing over a thousand pounds, that act like giant hammers," Lindsey told the fascinated group, "crushing even further the ore that has been mixed with water, and to which quicksilver is added. When it is fine enough, like sand, and looks like muddy water, it is known as slurry, and is passed through a screen and over an amalgam plate that, before the mill is started, is cleaned with cyanide and coated with silver nitrate and quicksilver. The quicksilver on the plate picks up the bright gold and silver by a process called amalgamation...."

For another ten minutes her voice droned on about the quicksilver trap, the percussion table, and the concentration tank, all further steps in the laborious process of removing gold from ore. She stopped short of getting into the refining of the gold.

"How much gold do you get per ton from this mine?" one of

the men asked.

"Anywhere from one-and-a-half to four ounces, which is quite respectable for this day, plus other minerals—namely silver and platinum. And to answer what is probably your next question, the mill can process ten tons of ore in a twenty-four hour period. We often keep it operating for ten-to-twenty days at a time, and it's scheduled to start up again late this afternoon."

Lindsey's eyes moved over the group but stopped when she came to J.L., who gave her a nod of respect for her knowledge and began to applaud, while the others heartily joined in. Lindsey smiled.

"I might add that mining costs are horrendous, so there isn't as much profit as one might expect, considering the figures I just gave you." She gestured around the area. "Most months we barely meet expenses and salaries."

She wished she could direct them to the small museum she had been working on for months, but it wasn't nearly ready for the public yet. There still remained a mountain of data and physical apparatus from the early days right up to the present to organize and display. Time and funds were the constant hindrances to the museum's completion.

"This ends our tour, ladies and gentlemen, but I'll be happy to answer any of your questions."

Some of the group headed for the parking lot and two men stayed behind to ask Lindsey more questions, which she easily answered, but there were none from J.L. He just stood there and watched her...and the men.

Later, when the tourists had gone away, but he had not, he walked with her to the mine office and Lindsey said, "I have to be leaving soon." In response to his raised eyebrows she explained, "I have an appointment with my attorney. Remember?"

"Yes, I do, and I hope it's not for a while yet, because we really do need to talk about this case against you."

Lindsey sighed impatiently and pushed ahead of him, ignoring his attempt to open the door to the office for her. Once inside, she retreated behind her desk and sank down into the old, squeaky chair.

J.L. sauntered into the office behind her, shrugged out of his suit jacket, dropped it on a nearby and dusty (she noticed with dismay) table, and loosened the knot in his tie—all movements that Lindsey found terribly appealing. His hands fascinated her. They were so deliberate, with a strong personality of their own as they moved from one task to another. She remembered the feel of those hands on her skin....

J.L. did not sit down, but stood in front of Lindsey's desk, those masculine hands at his sides, and went right to the heart of the matter: "Did you find the Full Reconveyance?"

"No, I didn't. Maybe my father destroyed it once the loan was paid back," she suggested, grasping at an unlikely straw, "or lost it."

J.L. shook his head no. "The county recorder would still have a record of the transaction. She doesn't. I inquired."

Lindsey smiled in defense. "I'm not going to worry about it because I know this is all a mistake."

"It's not a mistake."

"It's a mistake that I shall straighten out in time."

"Just so you realize there is a time limit."

Despite her nonchalant attitude, she knew very well that this was a serious problem, even though a part of her refused to believe what was happening: her world was crumbling around her, the light disappearing just as it did whenever she entered the mine.

She unsnapped the top button on her red paisley blouse and folded up the cuffs of the long sleeves. She was feeling claustrophobic in her own office.

J.L. silently watched every movement. He liked watching and listening to Lindsey Faraday. She was a lethal combination of brains and beauty—someone to respect and learn from, someone to take in his arms and kiss as he suspected she had never been kissed before.

He wondered how long he could keep from doing that. Not until the legal matter was settled, he had decided, but it would be tough waiting. So tough, in fact, that he had prayed about it just that morning. He had asked the Lord to give him the strength to do the right thing.

"Did my father and Francesca Owens know each other well?" Lindsey asked.

"My client has a diary in which her mother admits to being in love with your father. How he felt about her is not revealed, and it's a mystery why Francesca Owens did not do anything when the loan came due and wasn't paid back."

"Maybe she never wanted the money back," Lindsey snapped. "If she truly cared for my father, do you think she'd be pleased with your forcing me to repay the loan now?"

"My client needs the money."

"And my employees need jobs!" Lindsey contended, suddenly standing up to face him. "They have families. Two of them have young children; one is expecting another baby. I have to—" She broke off when emotion choked her, and she struggled to regain composure. Finally she said in a low voice, "Never mind. I'll work things out myself." She hugged herself at the waist and stared at the floor.

"Will you?" J.L.'s words were soft. He wanted to tell her there was another Source Who could help her.

"Yes," she said, forcing herself to calm down. "I've taken care of my people until now. I'll continue to do so, somehow, with God's help."

J.L.'s eyes opened wide. "Are you a Christian, Lindsey?"

"As of a few months ago."

He smiled. "Then trust in God to guide you. You're part of His family now…His child. He cares what happens to you."

Lindsey looked into J.L.'s eyes, more distressed than relieved to learn that they shared a common faith. If he was also a Christian, how could he be threatening her livelihood as he was? And if God was indeed her Heavenly Father, could she trust Him to always care for her?

She had trusted her father implicitly, believed him when he said everything he did was for her. Well, he had done one thing that was turning out not to be good for her at all. Would God be more reliable?

"I'm more concerned here for my employees than I am for myself," she told J.L. "I don't want anyone else but me running the mine."

"You're assuming that new owners would want to bring in their own people."

"It's a strong possibility, wouldn't you say? Especially with Santiago, at his age."

"Perhaps."

J.L. put his hands down on the desk and leaned forward. A nagging feeling was being born that told him she couldn't pay the thirty thousand dollars. Having seen the mine, its buildings, equipment, and environs, he suspected the Lucky Dollar was barely paying for itself and its employees. Could he really take it away from her, even for his client?

He respected her reluctance to simply take his word for the loan's having been made and not repaid. Thirty thousand dollars was a lot to give up when one wasn't certain that one had to. Even the legal documents he had had hadn't convinced her.

He wanted to help her, but couldn't. He represented someone else.

"You won't be losing your home in Majestic if the mine is sold, will you?" he asked, genuinely concerned.

She shook her head. "No, but Santiago has a simple cabin on the edge of the property that he's lived in for more than thirty years. I couldn't stand to see him lose it."

"Then just pay the thirty thousand dollars, Lindsey, and no one has to lose a job or a home."

Easier said than done, Lindsey could have said, but didn't. She still wasn't about to let J.L. Brett know she didn't have that kind of money. If it turned out she did have to repay the loan, perhaps some miracle would come along in the months before the foreclosure. The banks might lend her the money; she had an excellent credit rating. The Mother Lode might be discovered in the Lucky Dollar. She might be struck by lightning and then it wouldn't matter at all.

In frustration, she stuffed her hands into the back pockets of her jeans and stared out through a nearby open window, past a few of her men who were getting the stamp mill ready for operation, and looked beyond to the rugged hills behind and above the mine.

It was May and the mountain air was losing its crispness to soft breezes, one of which now floated into the room and fanned the heat of her cheeks.

Wild flowers filled the surrounding hills—golden California poppies, vibrant pink rose mallows, blue cowslips and lupine, yellow and purple and white blossoms bobbing on slender stalks, scattered in kaleidoscopic profusion over rocky ground that one would not think could grow anything. But they were there, hardy, returning every year, brilliant, scented, and presenting a dazzling contrast to the bleakness of the mine and the land around it.

The earth was alive with spring while her way of life could very well die.

Lindsey had to get outside, into the clean air, where she could breathe, look up and see the sky, while her eye could travel three-hundred-and-sixty degrees and see only her property…her property.

"Excuse me," she mumbled to J.L. as she rushed past him

and out the door. She practically ran along the gravel path, up the hill, paying no attention to Snooks and Bones, the mongrel dogs, who now gamboled around her feet so that she almost tripped on them.

When she reached the field of flowers, she threw herself down in them, sitting cross-legged, and smelled their perfume, and fought the tears.

She could hear the voices of Santiago and Larry shouting to each other by the stamp mill, and saw the mine and its rambling buildings and machinery below in the near distance. Why did she love it so? It was dirty and ugly and demanded far too much hard work for the little reward that it gave.

But it was her heart and soul, giving her treasured memories of her father and their days together. It was challenge and heartbreak, stubborn but with a rare burst of generosity such as the significant vein they had found just two years before.

To give it up willingly, to move on to another life, another endeavor, to marry Lance Robards, would be one thing. But to have the mine ripped from her against her will, would take her very life along with it.

She let out a long, slow sigh and leaned back on her elbows, stretching her legs out and closing her eyes, feeling the sun's warmth seep into her skin. The wind gently lifted the ends of her hair. She absorbed the absolute peace of the place in an effort to still her heart from surging to and fro for solutions.

She heard J.L. settle down in the flowers beside her, knew he was near her, but she did not open her eyes.

eleven

"Is this your special place?" J.L. asked.

Lindsey nodded silently, not wanting to put words to the truth that she had many times sought out this hill, this bumpy ground, this glorious expanse of sparse grass and stones and flowers that belonged to her.

"I have one, too. It's on the beach, about a mile from my house in La Jolla, a crescent-shaped stretch of sand that's hidden by shrubs and boulders." He sighed deeply. "My soul expands in that place when I feel the wind whip over my face and the salt spray get on my skin, and I can taste the ocean. I feel God there, in His nature."

Lindsey slowly opened her eyes, sat up, and turned her head to look at him. She knew what he meant about sensing God somewhere other than in church. She felt His strength in the rugged depths of her mine, His caring in the delicate wildflowers that beautified this very hill.

She wanted to ask J.L. about his faith, but she was hesitant to. It was all so new to her, and she had much to learn, but she didn't know if she should ask questions of the man who might destroy her golden dreams.

He was sitting there with one leg stretched out in front of him, the other bent, his arms leaning over his knee, and he was staring at the sign that hung above the entrance to the mine. It wasn't much of a sign, she had to admit, just a hunk of wood that someone a long time ago had carved with block letters announcing the location of the Lucky Dollar.

"It's the last mine around here, you know," she said in a voice that was faraway, as though she were talking to the wind instead of to him. "There were at least twenty-five of them in Majestic in the 1870s. What a boom town it was. The Lucky Dollar was the best."

He glanced at her. "In what way?"

"It's yielded almost four million dollars during the past century, but there's a whole lot more gold and silver in her, just waiting to be dug or blasted out."

Unwanted twin tears escaped her clouded eyes and zigzagged down her cheeks as she was overwhelmed with how much the mine and the men who worked it meant to her. She started to brush the tears away, but J.L. was there already, one of his fingers gently catching the tears as they fell.

"There's nothing wrong with caring," he said softly, his eyes soothing her with their understanding. His touch made her feel better, protected somehow, as though he understood how she felt, and approved.

She returned his look, and her heart slowed in anticipation, as he leaned over her and his fingers held her chin. Then she felt the moistness of his mouth when, after long exquisite seconds, he kissed her gently, like a feather touching velvet.

The kiss was sensitive and J.L. stayed against her mouth, savoring the sweet nectar of her lips, almost unbelieving of her willingness to share this sublime moment when their hearts touched.

He thought it would end soon, that she would push him away, but what he felt was a tremble that fluttered from her lips to his, and an almost inaudible murmur of satisfaction.

The kiss ended, but only long enough for them to gaze into each other's eyes with wonder, and then his arms reached out and gathered her against him, and a new kiss, one of more depth, took the place of the first and built in intensity as his lips searched for yet more of her sweetness.

He felt her hand grip his shoulder, then plunge into the thickness of his hair, and his hand tightened at her waist.

The thunderous sound of two, thousand-pound stamps suddenly roaring into action, beginning to crush a ton of ore beneath them, jolted Lindsey and J.L. apart. They sat bolt upright in their field of flowers, and stared down at the massive machinery.

When J.L.'s heart began to slow, he laughed outright. "I thought it was an earthquake," he admitted, running an unsteady hand through his thick shock of hair.

Lindsey grinned and yelled above the noise, "I thought your kiss had moved the earth for me."

They laughed together then, until J.L. thoughtfully gazed at her and, with a feather-light touch, stroked her forehead with the back of his fingers. "May I move the earth again?"

Lindsey, blushing, shook her head no and turned away from him, pointing down the hill. "Santiago probably started the mill to protect me."

J.L. grinned, disappointed with her decision, but knowing she was right. What had he been thinking of, kissing her that way? "Yes, he is staring at us, isn't he? I'm disappointed he thinks you need protection from me."

"It is a little silly since I'm a grown woman and can take care of myself."

"I'm sure you can." J.L. reached down and pulled from the ground a delicate pink blossom that he planned to place behind Lindsey's right ear. But his action was checked by the rambunctious interruption of Snooks and Bones, bounding up to them. The two dogs, one weighing a healthy forty pounds and the other a skinny brown runt worthy of his name Bones, were rewarded for their persistence when J.L. scratched their ears and wrestled with them, ignoring the damage they were doing to his suit pants. He petted them with a man's firm hands, which they adored and demanded more of.

Lindsey watched him, admitting to herself what an incredibly attractive man he was in many ways, with his deep, rich voice that mesmerized, his dimpled smile, and his generosity in representing people who could not afford attorney fees. He was even kind to animals. Still, was that any reason to lose her head over him? Absolutely not!

The sad truth was that she suspected she already had lost her head over him, or was fast on her way to doing so.

"You're spoiling my dogs," she said.

"I'd rather spoil their mistress," J.L. countered, rising to his feet and extending a hand to help her up, too, which she accepted.

"I don't need spoiling. I need to be left alone, with my life intact."

"Lindsey, I'd love to do that, but I can't. Facts are facts." He kept her hand and started them down the hill, the dogs following, but then Lindsey pulled away from him, knowing she had crossed a dangerous line when she had let him kiss her. She had never intended to do that, and all the reasons why she could not get close to J.L. Brett came flooding into her mind, allowing her to put up an emotional wall between them.

"You don't trust me, do you?" he asked.

"Should I?"

"Of course you should."

"You're asking too much. I don't know you or what kind of man you are. What makes you tick. Why are you a champion of the unfortunate when there's no money in it?"

"Is this curiosity about a man you're starting to care about?"

Lindsey forced out a breath. "No, Mr. Brett. It's just an explanation of why I won't care about you."

"Even if I tell you why I am the man I am?"

"No." She meant it. She had been foolish to give in to his kisses, to let him rouse her feelings. They were in combat. She had to stand against him, not melt into his arms.

They were back down the hill now and walking toward the

lot where J.L.'s truck was parked.

"I was beaten up when I was six years old," he started, despite her not wanting him to, "because I wouldn't voluntarily give my lunch money to an older boy. I did not enjoy the experience, and I never forgot it. When I was ten, and big for my age, I went after some boys who had taken the football of a friend of mine, a Mexican boy who was little. I won because of my size. In junior high my opponents also were big, but this time I won by using my brain to defend a new girl who was being taunted because of her red hair."

Lindsey couldn't help being intrigued. "What did you do?"

"Not do...say. I lied through my teeth and told the bullies that her dad was the police chief and ate junior highers for breakfast, none of which was true, but I learned something: brains can be more effective than brawn in getting what you want. That's when I decided I enjoyed helping people who could not help themselves."

Lindsey murmured, "And did all these friends properly appreciate your help?" She could just see him on a white horse, riding to the rescue of the beautiful redhead in distress, who then lavished him with grateful kisses.

"The girl gave me a whole bag of homemade chocolate chip cookies...one of the best payments I've ever received."

A rush of admiration made Lindsey silently study J.L. Brett for a moment. "Does your present client have red hair?" she asked softly, admitting that the world needed attorneys who cared about bringing justice to those who couldn't obtain it for themselves.

J.L. leaned back against the door of the truck, grinned, and shook his head no, and Lindsey wished he were defending her instead of persecuting her. It would be better to have him on her side.

With grudging appreciation, she gazed into his eyes and he returned her gaze, their smiles slowly disappearing as velvet thoughts about each other moved into their heads, thoughts that saw good more than bad and gave birth to respect that went beyond physical attraction.

"If I don't hurry, I'll be late for my appointment with my lawyer," she said.

J.L. nodded, approving. Maybe if she heard the facts from another attorney, she would believe it and they could get the matter settled. "Do remember," he said to her, "that you need to decide soon what you're going to do."

There it was, the gentle threat, and Lindsey didn't like the sound of it. "All right, all right," she replied sharply, "I understand. Would the amount have to be paid all at once?"

"Yes."

Her breath quickened. "And if I don't?"

"Then I file a Notice of Default with the county."

"After which?"

"You'll have a three-month reinstatement period to cure the default. If you fail to do that, public notice will be given and the mine will be sold to the highest bidder."

Lindsey whirled around, her back to J.L. She felt sick to her stomach.

So it was over, the dance between them, the vying for position, like two wrestlers circling each other, waiting for their first chance to contact. She had tried to avoid the situation, denying its existence. She had tried to avoid J.L. Brett, the man, but had failed at that, too.

She had kissed him, had been in his arms, had felt for one or two crazy moments that he really cared for her. Didn't he? If so, it didn't deter him from doing his job of getting a whole lot of money from her for his client. The most frightening thought was that J.L. Brett did not strike her as the kind of man who would waste his time on a case that wasn't foolproof.

She was going to have to fight for the Lucky Dollar with every means she had, and she would before she'd just hand it over, but the idea of repaying thirty thousand dollars was about as possible as California never again having an earthquake.

"There's one thing you should know about me," Lindsey said, turning around and looking J.L. straight in the eye. "I honor my commitments; I pay my debts. If, and I say *if* this debt of my father's is legitimate, then it shall be paid, no matter what it takes to do so. But, if this proves to be just somebody's idea of a way to get their hands on some quick money, you are going to have the fight of your life on your hands. Do you understand, Mr. Brett?"

J.L. gave her a rakish grin. "Yes, ma'am."

Lindsey spun around and strode away, back along the path toward the office, and shouted over her shoulder, "I'll be in touch." She longed for J.L. to follow her, stop her, take her in his arms and tell her there had been a terrible mistake, that she was safe, her mine was safe, her workers were safe.

But instead, she walked on, and heard the sound of J.L.'s truck starting up. Slowly it moved out of the parking lot, the big tires mercilessly crunching the gravel beneath them, and Lindsey kept walking until she got to the office. Inside, she threw herself into her chair behind her desk, put her head down on her arms, and wept.

twelve

I'm a fool to jeopardize my objectivity by falling for Lindsey Faraday, J.L. told himself as he drove away from the mine, but he knew he was drawn to her goodness, her determination, and that innocent, soft beauty that with one look melted his rough edges.

His euphoria at having held Lindsey in his arms was still fresh in his mind, as was the taste of her lips on his. Yet, an unwanted suspicion crept into his brain: *Did she give herself to me so I would ease up on the legal case and persuade my client to drop the demand?*

"No!" he said out loud. "Lindsey's not that kind of woman. I know that! I know that? I've been with her only three times. That hardly makes me an expert on the workings of her mind and heart."

He pounded the steering wheel with the heel of one hand and decided he had better watch his step before he made a crucial error in handling this case for his client.

❧

By the time Lindsey lifted her head from her desk, it was nearly dark. The sky outside was gray and the stamp mill was still making horrendous noise as it went about its job of grinding rock into dust.

She stood up, hastily wiped the now-dried tears from her face, went outside, and said good night to Santiago and the men. Then she drove to her little house in Majestic, determined to forget what had happened between herself and J.L. Brett.

While she could not satisfactorily explain why she had kissed him, and enjoyed it, one thing she knew for certain: she was not interested in a quick fling or having an affair. She looked forward to a physical relationship with a man, but she wanted it only in marriage, surrounded by commitment and genuine caring.

She did not know, of course, how J.L. felt about such things. He seemed to be a Christian, so perhaps he shared her ideals, but she didn't know him well enough to be sure. What if kissing her had been nothing more than a pleasant diversion for him, or a way to soften her attitude and eventually benefit his client? That horrible doubt locked into Lindsey's mind and taunted her while she drove right through a stop sign.

"Dear Lord, I need Your guidance," she prayed. "I'm not experienced in the ways of men. I haven't dated anyone for quite a while, and now I have Lance wanting to marry me but my heart is responding to J.L. Help me, God, to make wise decisions."

Arriving home, she picked up the evening paper on the front porch, and went inside her two-bedroom, one-storied house that had been there for over forty years. She tossed her purse on the couch and sank down into her favorite chair to glance at the headlines, but her mind was not on current events. She was drowning in a sea of contradictory feelings for J.L. Brett.

She didn't want to be with him, but she did. They weren't right for each other because they were so different. He was a brainy lawyer. She worked with her hands, in dirt. He made his living by the power of his words, persuading jurors and judges to his way of thinking. She was a worker, not a talker, and was not at all clever at bantering words with aggressive men.

He was experienced with women. That was obvious from the way he touched her. She, on the other hand, was relatively inexperienced with men. He roused strange new feelings in her that were as dangerous as dynamite ready to explode, and because Lindsey knew she couldn't avoid being with him, she also knew she could get emotionally hurt.

How can I protect myself? she asked herself as she took a shower, changed clothes, and waited for the only lawyer in town, who happened to be a friend of hers, to come to the house for their appointment. She really needed his help.

≥≈

John Gregory, tall, lanky, thirty-eight years old, and balding, looked at the copies of the Note and Deed of Trust that Lindsey handed him. "These appear to be in order, but they aren't proof the loan wasn't repaid. I'll check with the county recorder's office. But I must tell you, Lindsey, if Jonathan Brett is against you, there's little chance of your winning the case."

"Why do you say that?"

"Because he has a reputation in the legal field for being tough and shrewd, also completely honest, and only takes on cases he totally believes in."

Lindsey sighed and poured them both glasses of iced tea. They were standing in her kitchen. "Is it true he likes to represent people who can't really afford a high-priced lawyer?"

"Yes. They say he works for pennies when he could get thousands from important people who want him every day of the week. He lets his associates handle the high-profile cases while he takes on the world for those who can't protect themselves."

"He sounds too good to be true," Lindsey grumbled, skeptical.

"He's a man of high principles."

"Who strikes me as being a maverick. I mean, John, how many lawyers do you know who go around dressed like Wild Bill Hickock?"

He chuckled. "He is different, I'll grant you. A throwback to a century ago, when he should have been born, so he could have tamed the West. He raises horses, I'm told, and would rather be riding in the hills than attending a social event."

Lindsey carried two small plates, on which sat store-bought chocolate cupcakes, into the cozy living room where she directed John to a long, comfortable-looking, ten-year-old couch upholstered in a faded floral pattern. Two imitation Tiffany lamps, on either end of the couch, cast a cheerful glow about the room, and Lindsey sat down in a cane-backed chair in front of the fireplace.

"Do you think this client he's representing is also highly principled, or just money grubbing and after my mine?" she asked him, taking a bite of the cupcake and licking the frosting off her lip with her tongue.

"From what I've been told, J.L. Brett won't be involved in anything that isn't strictly on the up and up."

Lindsey's heart sank. "Isn't there a loophole somewhere, John? A statute of limitations or something that will keep Mr. Brett's client from foreclosing on the Lucky Dollar?"

"I'll try to find one."

"Please let me know the minute you have any information for me."

"Will do." He finished the cupcake, wiped his fingers on the napkin, and stood up. "How about dinner one night this week?"

Lindsey knew he had feelings for her. He spoke to her every time they ran into each other in town, and had even asked her out a few times. She had always said no, and he had accepted rejection as a gentleman, but she wondered if he would think her coming to him now was an open door to something personal developing. She hoped not. It was all she could do now to cope with the threat to the mine, the pressure of Lance Robards to deepen their relationship, and her irrational feelings for J.L. Brett.

"I think I'll pass on the dinner, John, but I do so appreciate your helping me. I'll expect a bill from you." She gave him a winning smile and walked him out to his car, satisfied that someone wiser than herself in matters like these was now on her side. She even allowed herself to feel optimistic that John would find the answer to saving her mine.

He drove away with a wave, and Lindsey gave a big sigh and

turned back to the home she had lived in for many years. It wasn't an impressive house by any means, just a square wooden building needing a fresh coat of pale green paint, with a small porch in the front, weeds growing up between the flagstones, and a little grass around its four sides.

The backyard was a good size. At one end of it was a building, misnamed a garage, that just barely accommodated her Jeep Cherokee and a lawn mower.

Inside, the house was welcoming, if not glamorous, and, while the decor might not thrill an interior decorator, there was a warmth and casualness about it that suited Lindsey just fine. "It's a house of character," she had often said proudly; that, translated, meant there were things that needed repair and furnishings that could just as easily have come from a yard sale as from a fancy department store.

More important than glamorous furnishings, she felt, was to be surrounded by things she treasured: a music box her father had given her on her twelfth birthday that played Brahms, an arrangement of silk flowers from Santiago, a picture of her and her father, in a silver frame, grinning over the largest gold nugget they had ever found in the Lucky Dollar.

There was no picture of her mother, Alicia, a world-renowned concert pianist, although Lindsey had several including an especially nice one showing her playing at the Royal Albert Hall in London, wearing a stunning, white satin evening gown. The picture was kept in a drawer, not on a shelf.

Lindsey pulled off her dusty cowboy boots and trudged wearily into the kitchen to wash the glasses and plates she and John had used, her feet relishing the rough feel of the well-trodden braided rug on the wooden floor. Whoever came up with the phrase, "Home Sweet Home," certainly knew what he or she was talking about, Lindsey decided. She loved her home, the natural acreage it was on, and the interesting small town in which it existed.

Above the sink were three black-and-white pictures of the

Lucky Dollar at the turn of the century. Lindsey paused in her dishwashing to gaze in adoration at the sights she had seen a hundred times before, but never tired of.

Her life had been a good one, filled with simple pleasures and simple friendships…hard work…some rewards. The thrill of being allowed to try, sometimes doing well, other times failing. But that was what it was all about—good days and bad days.

Outside, a few male cicadas began their night singing, and Lindsey finished her chore and went back into the living room where she collapsed onto the comfy old couch and took off the end table the large Bible she had bought the week before, from which she read a few chapters every evening. Instead of opening the book right away, she clasped it against her chest and closed her eyes.

"There is so much about You I don't know," she prayed to God in a whisper. "I know this is Your Word to me. Give me the desire to read it and help me to understand why You love me and want me for Your child. This Bible tells me You are my Father, and that You want to give me abundant life, and that if I will acknowledge You and trust You, You will direct my paths."

Lindsey gazed up at the picture of her father and her on the fireplace mantel. "I had a wonderful father, Lord. He loved me more than anything, and took care of me, and gave me a wonderful life. But now he's gone, and he's left me a problem I need to solve."

Lindsey's eyes filled with tears. Her heart ached from missing her father. If any child ever adored and trusted a father, she had hers. William Faraday had been her whole world.

"My father's gone, dear Lord, but I have You." Lindsey smiled as an unusual peace settled over her. She tucked her feet under her and rested her head on the back of the couch, letting her thoughts roam, over her life, her family, the mine, her friends, J.L. Brett. They stopped with him, with a recollection of dark, probing eyes but a happy, dimpled smile that could make her forget the harsh realities of life.

She wondered about love. What exactly was it? Did she need it to be complete? Her father had loved her mother, once, and look at the pain he had suffered. Lindsey had decided very young that man/woman love was not as important as people claimed it was.

So, when J.L. had taken her into his arms, and kissed her, she had been surprised at how much she had liked it, and how far different his kisses were from those few Lance had given her.

Lance was a passionate man, and so was J.L., but Lance seemed intent on pleasing himself, whereas J.L. had approached her with more tenderness, more in exploration as to what would please her as well as himself.

"I can't think of him," she said out loud. "I won't think of him," and she fell asleep, still clutching the Bible in her hands, while the world outside darkened and surrounded her house. Inside, though, she was warm and protected, for the moment.

❧

The days went by, a week exactly, and then Lindsey heard from John. "I couldn't find anything to show that the loan was ever repaid, Lindsey. I'm afraid Brett's client has legal claim to thirty thousand of your dollars."

Lindsey didn't cry; she just went dead inside. "Thank you, John," she said quietly and hung up the phone.

For days after that phone call, she hardly said a word to anyone, and the men at the mine worried about her.

She knew she had to call J.L. and tell him the situation, and she did try to do so, several times, but every time her hand reached for the phone, she felt sick to her stomach and just couldn't do it. It would be like digging her own grave.

Another week went by, a week of agony when all she could think of was losing the Lucky Dollar. She also couldn't stop thinking of J.L., her thoughts being a crazy mixture of good memories and bad. He was two sides of a coin to her, one where she'd win, the other where she'd lose.

She really expected him to call or come to see her, but he didn't, and she wondered why. How long would he wait for her to contact him?

Had she been right in figuring he didn't take their romantic interlude seriously, or was he backing away from the case because he didn't want to hurt her?

She hated all the mental gymnastics she was going through these days and longed for times past when running the mine had been her only concern. Oh, what she wouldn't give for her life to be like that again, with her father alive, and them sharing their hopes for the future.

It was on a day when Lindsey already had a headache that the official-looking envelope arrived from the county. Tearing it open with dread, Lindsey's worst nightmare came true: a Notice of Default had been filed with the county by the law firm of Brett and Associates. She had ninety days to pay J.L.'s client thirty thousand dollars. If she did not, the mine would be sold.

He didn't even wait for me to tell him whether or not I could pay the money, she at first fumed, but then had to admit he had given her more than enough time to contact him. Only she hadn't, and he had acted.

Leaping to her feet, she slammed the letter down on the desk. "He didn't have the common decency to let me know he was going to file," she grumbled out loud. "The snake in the grass. The despicable snake in the grass. Well, he can't do this to me!" and she stormed out of the office, ignoring the dogs as well as the cheerful greeting of Santiago as he passed by her.

Her foreman stopped and watched Lindsey plunge, stone-faced, down the path toward her Jeep. *Someone's in a whole lot of trouble,* he thought, and just knew it was J.L. Brett.

thirteen

Lindsey did not obey the speed limit in driving the sixty miles southwest to San Diego. Later she would berate herself for being foolish, but now all she could think of was seeing J.L. Brett, face to face, and telling him a thing or two.

Don't lose your temper, she told herself, concerned over a trait she had battled all her life and had been praying, since her conversion, would come under God's control. *Temper never solves anything. Just ask J.L. Brett how a man can hold a woman in his arms one day and then legally move to take away her livelihood the next?*

Fortunately, it wasn't rush hour as she distractedly drove her sturdy Jeep through the downtown, area looking for Fifth Avenue where many prestigious businesses were located, and for the building in which the arch villain, J.L. Brett, worked.

She breezed, unseeing, through the sophisticated lobby, rode the silent elevator to the top floor while rehearsing just what she was going to say to a certain lawyer. She stepped out into a magnificent reception area of walnut woods, beveled mirrors, and oriental flower arrangements, but she was barely aware of her surroundings. Her thinking was focused on one thing only—confronting J.L. Brett.

He had betrayed her. He had kissed her in a way she had never been kissed, scratched the ears of her dogs, and then walked away to file his contemptible Notice of Default.

He deserved to know just what she thought of him. *Just don't lose your temper,* she warned herself one last time.

"I'd like to see J.L. Brett," she stated to a middle-aged receptionist who answered politely, "Your name, please?"

"Lindsey Faraday."

"I'll see if Mr. Brett is in."

Lindsey felt like charging down the twin halls that led to the right and left away from the reception area, banging on every door until she found the scoundrel. But she was, after all, she told herself, a civilized person, with manners, and she would not be rude to J.L.'s employees when it was the man himself who would receive her indignation.

The receptionist hung up the phone, gave Lindsey a sincere smile, and said, "If you'll take the hallway to your right, Miss Faraday, Mr. Brett's office is at the end of it."

Lindsey took a quick breath and said, "Thank you." Then she covered the distance in record time and burst through the door.

A stunning young woman with sleek, raven hair pulled back in an attractive chignon rose from behind a large oak desk, the top of which was unbelievably uncluttered. Her skin was flawless, her nails expertly polished, and her stylish suit showed nary a wrinkle.

"Miss Faraday?" she asked with cool appraisal.

"Yes." Lindsey moved swiftly to the desk. "I'd like to see J.L., please."

Heather Davenport eyed Lindsey's yellow Wrangler jeans, simple yellow blouse under a brown suede jacket with fringed sleeves, and well-worn brown boots that left no doubt she worked in the out-of-doors, far from the city. Was her style of dress what Mr. Brett had meant when he had said she was "different"?

Heather came around her desk to stand closer to Lindsey, and saw shining golden hair, vivid blue eyes, soft skin. She knew then Mr. Brett's terse comment involved more than a physical assessment. There was something palpable about Lindsey Faraday, an intensity that blended with an unmistakable naivete that would always cause someone to give her a second look.

"I'm Heather Davenport, Miss Faraday, Mr. Brett's executive secretary."

Lindsey's gaze shot to the double doors behind the secretary's desk. "Is *he* in there?" She said the pronoun as though J.L. were a runaway plague.

Heather knew her duty, and acted on it. "Mr. Brett is not able to see you now, Miss Faraday."

Lindsey glanced down at the telephone board. One of the lines was lit up. "I'll take only a moment of his time, Miss Davenport," and before Heather could stop her, she surged forward, flung open one of the doors with only a quick knock. There he was, the snake.

"Bingo," she cried out.

J.L. glanced up as Lindsey charged into the room. "I'll call you back," he said into the phone, and started to get up, but Lindsey was already there, behind his desk, with her hands on his shoulders, pushing him back into his chair.

"Is something wrong?" he asked, not mistaking the sparks in her eyes that resembled a volcano about to erupt.

"Now why would you think that, J.L., just because you filed a Notice of Default against my mine?"

"You knew I had to do that sooner or later, Lindsey. I waited as long as I could."

"Did you?"

He started to get up, but she pushed him back down.

Heather, still standing at the door, unable to tear herself away from the drama unfolding, sprang forward and asked, "Mr. Brett, shall I call security?"

J.L. glared at her as though she were daft. Security? She thought he needed protection from a hundred and twenty pounds of soft woman, albeit a woman who was bent on intimidation? "No security, Heather. Just close the door behind you when you leave."

Heather reluctantly made her exit but stayed on the other side of the door, her ear to the wood. She had never seen anyone treat J.L. Brett that way and her curiosity demanded she learn all she could about the situation.

"You really are something else," Lindsey leaned over him to within inches of his face. "First you tell me I'm beautiful—"

He thinks she's beautiful? Heather frowned.

"Then you kiss me among the flowers—"

Flowers? On the ground? Heather clasped a hand over her mouth to stifle an exclamation.

"Then you have the unbelievable gall to file a Notice of Default on me when you know I'm trying to find proof that that ridiculous loan was paid back. You tried to soften me up so I'd give your client the money without a fuss."

"That's not true, Lindsey." J.L. slid the chair back on the plastic mat and rose to his feet, towering over her, his expression concerned. "Holding you in my arms had nothing to do with the legal problem between us."

"Didn't it?"

"Have you forgotten that we both felt the earth move?"

Heather gasped.

"It was just a game you were playing with me, wasn't it...the passionate kisses?"

"Oh," Heather moaned. She had been yearning for three years for J.L. to kiss her passionately, or any other way.

"I wouldn't play games with your emotions, Lindsey. I'm not that kind of man."

"Ah yes, I know of your sterling reputation as a man of principle." She leaned toward him. "But maybe people don't know you as well as they think they do."

J.L.'s eyes darkened. "I'm sorry this is hard on you, Lindsey, but the law is the law. Your father borrowed money; it has to be repaid. End of case."

He reached out to her, but she backed away, around the

corner of his desk, past a well-worn western saddle and lariat that had once belonged to Will Rogers. With her hands firmly planted on her hips, she said, "You'd do anything to get what you want for your client, wouldn't you?"

"If you're saying I manipulate people, you're wrong, Lindsey."

"I don't think so. You're unethical."

Heather's eyes widened.

J.L. reached out and grasped Lindsey's hand.

She struggled to be free. "Let me go, you brute."

Heather gulped.

"Not until you calm down."

"I'm never going to calm down because you…you are unscrupulous as well as unethical."

"Hey, wait a minute."

"And dishonest."

"Whoa!" J.L. felt heat around his collar.

"You should be reported to the Bar Association."

"Miss Faraday, you're out of line."

"I have a right to be. You used me."

"I kissed you and you responded."

Heather ground her teeth.

"If you don't let go of me within five seconds, J.L. Brett, you'll be sorry."

"I said I'm not going to let you go until you calm down so we can talk about this rationally."

Lindsey kicked him in the shins.

"Ow," he howled.

Heather's eyebrows shot up.

"You're crazy, you know that?" He leaned over and rubbed his legs. "This isn't the way differences are solved by mature adults."

"I'm just defending what is mine," Lindsey declared as she whirled around and started for the door.

J.L. limped after her. "Just pay the stupid money," he yelled.

Lindsey stopped, turned, and stared at him. *He's lost his temper,* she thought in amazement. Then she smiled smugly. *I'm so glad I didn't lose mine.*

Since she was in total control of herself, she now looked around J.L.'s office. It was spacious, decorated with deep-seated chairs and a couch, rugged oak furniture, and cowboy memorabilia sprawled on tables and shelves. Through the huge window behind his desk she saw a breathtaking view of sunny San Diego. Hanging on the walls were oil and watercolor paintings of forests and waterfalls and Half Dome in Yosemite, portraying the personal likes of this man who loved the outdoors.

It was a sumptuous office, expensively furnished, and far different from her dilapidated one at the mine. Lindsey wondered if it would make any difference if she told J.L. the reason she wasn't paying the money immediately to his client was that she barely had thirty thousand dollars in the bank and that some of that was retirement money for her employees, which she would never touch.

No, he wouldn't understand, she decided, *not with all the money he obviously has if this office is any indication. Thirty thousand dollars probably means nothing to him, but giving that much away is an impossibility for me.*

Frustration at being hounded ended Lindsey's speculation and renewed her determination to fight the injustice being thrust upon her. She bravely stepped closer to J.L., looked up into his blazing eyes, and issued an ultimatum: "You tell your nameless client to meet me in court, Mr. Brett. This whole thing is a setup. There never was a loan."

"What?" J.L. raged. "Are you accusing me of being party to a deception?"

"Why not?"

"You're loony. Irrational."

Heather's mouth was agape. She had never heard J.L. so

upset. "You put that down, Lindsey," she heard him warn.

Lindsey had picked up a cloisonnè vase and was holding it between her hands. It was cool and elegant. It belonged to J.L. Brett. She wanted to throw it. Needed to throw it. Shouldn't throw it. She desperately wanted to control her temper, but she was growing angrier by the moment and her body demanded she do something physical to relieve its tension.

"Don't you throw that," J.L. warned, starting menacingly toward her. "That would be childish, unproductive, and—"

She threw it.

"Ridiculous!" he roared.

Heather quaked at the door.

The vase shattered into three large pieces and a dozen smaller ones, and Lindsey felt infinitely better.

"You're going to pay for that," J.L. shouted at her, his face rigid.

"You'll get that the same day you get my mine," Lindsey yelled back. She yanked open the door to leave his office and ran over, literally, Heather, who was leaning on the other side of it.

The secretary scrambled as fast as she could to get out of the path of Lindsey's tornado exit. Good thing, for J.L. didn't see her there and slammed the door. A huge, glass-framed picture that hung behind her desk, on the same wall as his office door, crashed to the floor.

Heather's suit was wrinkled. Her hair was mussed. She had broken a fingernail. But she had heard it all and still couldn't believe it. Even though Mr. Brett had told Lindsey Faraday that she was beautiful and he had kissed her passionately among the flowers, she had kicked him in the shins and broken a priceless vase. Heather sank down onto the chair behind her desk and decided that this fiery young woman was Enemy Number One and would never get by her again.

fourteen

The morning after her confrontation with J.L., Lindsey felt utter shame. How could she have stormed into his office that way, confronted him so rudely, accused him of unethical conduct, and then smashed an expensive vase? How could she have lost her temper when she had been so determined not to lose it?

I guess this is what the Bible calls being a carnal Christian, she thought while listlessly buttering a piece of cold toast in her kitchen, *doing things you don't want to do and not doing things you should do. I hope there's an answer for it in the Scriptures.*

She poured milk into a bowl of cornflakes, added some banana slices, and ate at her kitchen table while staring out the window at the riot of daffodils that grew along a broken-down wooden fence. Now she understood the Old Testament story spoken by the prophet Nathan about a man who had only one little lamb, his children's pet, and was forced to give it to a rich man who had guests to feed but wouldn't take from his own many flocks to do so.

J.L. Brett and his ruthless client were trying to take what little she had, and she couldn't let them do that—not just for her sake, but for the sakes of those conscientious, deserving men who worked for her, and especially Santiago, who had given three decades of his life to the Lucky Dollar.

Still, I shouldn't have lost my temper, and I was rude to J.L.'s receptionist and secretary, she thought as she washed the few dishes she had used for her breakfast. *What a mannerless creature they must think me to be.* So, before going to the mine, she wrote them both a warm note of apology, which shocked Heather, who never mentioned it to J.L.

Life moved on. Lindsey's bank turned down her request for a loan. She applied at another and another, with no success. The fourth bank, in the next county, was in no hurry to make a decision and Lindsey struggled to maintain hope.

Could she ask for help from her talented and wealthy mother? No, for Alicia Faraday had never shown much interest in Lindsey, not even wanting custody of her when the divorce had taken place. Yes, they spoke to each other once or twice a year, usually by phone, but only rarely had Lindsey seen her mother in person, and she had too much pride to turn to her now.

How about her maternal grandmother? Unfortunately, they were not close enough for her to ask such a huge favor since her Grandmother Mathis blamed the breakup of her daughter's marriage on William Faraday for wanting a silly gold mine and giving up a lucrative career in a prestigious stock brokerage to get it. She conveniently ignored the fact that her daughter had a dream, also, to play the piano, around the world, away from her family.

What am I to do? Lindsey pondered day after day. Her responsibility for her employees, and especially Santiago and his wife, Maria, weighed heavily on her, and a solution eluded her.

She remembered J.L.'s words more than once: "Trust in God to guide you. You're part of His family now…His child. He cares what happens to you."

She wanted to trust. She was trying to trust, but the waiting was hard.

Lance was not as sympathetic as she had hoped he would be when she told him of the situation one night when they were having dinner at one of his restaurants.

"Maybe it's meant to be…that you'll have to sell the mine. Then you can marry me and be free of that responsibility."

Lindsey frowned. "It's a joy, not a responsibility, Lance, and I don't want to be free of it. Even if I have to sell it, I would still wish I were running it."

"I don't understand that." He played with the fine hairs of his blond moustache.

"I know." The tiny hope that had come to mind while they were eating, that Lance might loan her the money, was extinguished.

"I love you, sweetheart," he said, reaching for her hand and raising her fingertips to his lips, "and admire your intelligence and spunk in running that dirty old mine, but that surely can't be something you want to do the rest of your life. You wouldn't want your children growing up around that dangerous place, would you?"

"Why not? I did and loved every minute of it. My father taught me to be careful, and gave me responsibility, and the miners took me under their wings—"

"That's another thing: I worry about you up in those hills, alone, with just a bunch of crusty old men around."

"You mustn't worry," she assured him. "They're my protectors as well my employees. Not one of them would ever hurt me."

"You don't know that."

"Yes, I do. I know my men. They're hard working and faithful and I'd trust them with my life."

Lance laid her hand down and reached inside his suit jacket. "It's just that I love you so much, Lindsey, I don't want anything to happen to you." He took something small from his shirt pocket and handed it to her. "Open it, sweetheart."

Lindsey hesitantly took the blue velvet box from him and slowly opened it, knowing what was inside, and she was right—it was a diamond ring, large and flashy and expensive, she was sure. It was pretty, she supposed, but it wasn't something she would have chosen for herself.

"Lance, you shouldn't have done this."

"Yes, I should have, and I know you haven't said yes to my proposal yet, but I'm an optimistic guy." He winked at her. "I know you will some day, and soon. I wanted you to see the ring, Lindsey, and think about it. Maybe it will help you make up your mind."

Lindsey just smiled, knowing she liked Lance and was enjoying getting to know him, but also knowing she was not at all sure their friendship would mature into love.

At home that night, reading her Bible before going to bed, she turned to the fifth and sixth verses of Proverbs 3 that she was trying to memorize: "Trust in the Lord with all thine heart; and lean not unto thine own understanding. In all thy ways acknowledge him, and he shall direct your paths."

She lifted her face upward and closed her eyes. "I know I'm your child now, Lord, and that You care for me. Help me to let You guide me, and not get in the way."

❧

It was six weeks after the episode at J.L.'s office, on a Sunday afternoon, six weeks that had tried Lindsey's patience and wits and had, despite her best efforts, made her snappish toward almost anyone who crossed her path.

The men stayed as far away from her as they could. Snooks and Bones ducked their heads and put their tails between their legs when Lindsey approached, having been yelled at a couple of times when they never had been before.

Even Santiago walked on eggs around her, and more than once Lindsey chided herself for a display of temper she seemed less and less able to control.

It was hard for her to relax, to greet each day with the joy and enthusiasm she once had, for there was no telling how long she would even own the Lucky Dollar.

"I trust You, Lord," she said every day, but that trust didn't manifest itself in her behavior.

When she asked her lawyer friend, John, to do her one more favor, to find out how much the Lucky Dollar was worth, there were tears in her eyes. "I guess I'm going to have to sell it," were the hardest words she had ever spoken.

Today, Lindsey was curled up on a wicker chair on her front porch, her bare feet tucked beneath her. She should have been at the mine an hour ago, but just hadn't been able to get herself going.

She wasn't daydreaming; she had given that up weeks before. She was still struggling with how she could repay her father's debt without having to sacrifice the mine.

Her mind in a whirl, her emotions frayed, she gazed over the peaceful slope of scrubby grass, tall pines, and rocky ground that made up the five acres of property she owned. She appreciated the fact that she had so much land. It gave her a peaceful, uncrowded life. But was it a complete life? The question suddenly came to her.

She listened to the quiet, to the leaves of the oak trees, rustling in the early morning breeze. No sound here of blaring music from a neighbor's stereo. No monotonous drone of cars on a freeway. No man talking to her, either, sharing his day and dreams.

Tears spilled over her cheeks as she remembered the wonderful talks she had had with her father, on this very porch, in this very chair. They had laughed together, planned together, shared the love of the Lucky Dollar. All this had given her a growing up she wouldn't trade with anyone else's.

She had been blessed to live in this simple place, learning to work hard and care deeply. The people she knew in Majestic were down-to-earth, honest folk, earning a living in a way they liked, not pressured to live up to someone else's standards. They weren't terribly sophisticated, but they were genuine. They didn't move fast, but they accomplished much in preserving a meaningful life that many of those people on the most prestigious streets in San Diego could only dream about.

She heard someone approaching, and looked up to see Santiago lumbering up the path, his shoulders sagging and his face wearing an expression of dejection.

"Hello, there," she called out to him. "Come sit. Can I get you some coffee?"

The old foreman shook his head no and gave her a half-smile as he sank down in the nearest chair.

"There isn't trouble at the mine, is there?" she asked.

"Nope. The mine's fine; the men are working. Larry is singing his fool head off 'cause his Susy is pregnant again. You know how he gets."

"Yes." Lindsey laughed, then sobered. "But something's wrong, Santiago. I can see it in your eyes."

"You're right." He fidgeted in the chair.

"Well, if it's not the mine or the men, what is it?"

"It's you, boss. Something's going on you're not telling me about, and I want to help." His words were filled with concern. "What can I do?"

Lindsey sighed and closed her eyes for a moment, then admitted, "I'm up against a stone wall, Santiago," and she told him everything about the loan, but not about kissing J.L. in the flowers and attacking him in his own law office.

Santiago frowned. "Don't you think I had a right to know about the mine, boss? After all, I've given my life for the Lucky Dollar."

Lindsey reached out and grasped both his hands. "The only reason I didn't tell you was that I didn't want you to worry about losing your job, and house, in case whoever buys the mine brings in his own people."

Her blue eyes misted with tears and she whimpered like a wounded animal, "Oh, Santiago, what am I going to do? I have less than two months to pay back J.L. Brett's client or I lose the mine. I have enough money in one account to satisfy the loan, but I've been saving that for my employees' retirement and it would be hard to build it up again before one of the men needs it. Also, I have a few thousand in a general account, but it's not enough and is earmarked for everyday expenses."

Santiago was quiet for a long time, thinking. "I never heard of your father getting such a loan," he said at last, "but we'll think of something to do 'cause I know the Lucky Dollar is your whole life, just as it was your daddy's. You've both been real good to me and Maria. You're like family."

Lindsey heard the pathos in his voice and wanted to hug him and assure him that everything would be all right. But she couldn't do that, for she had no idea of how to get out of the terrible trouble she was in.

fifteen

In the law office of Brett and Associates, things were not much better than at the Lucky Dollar. For weeks J.L. had been like a wounded bull—cross, abrupt, a perpetual scowl on his face, giving sharp orders to Heather and little more than grunts to his associates.

"Mr. Brett is getting on my nerves," Angela Baines said to Heather. Angela handled all the tax cases for the firm and was normally calm, deliberative, and never raised her voice. She was thirty-nine years old, extremely intelligent, married to a pediatrician, and had been with J.L. for five years. She had never seen him in this state of mind.

"He's normally not moody," Heather defended her boss.

"He's moody now."

"Or temperamental."

"He's temperamental now."

Heather suspected the reason was because of that scrawny mine owner who had gotten him to make passionate love to her in a field of flowers. Despite Lindsey's hand-written apology note, Heather thought her little better than an unsophisticate.

Angela's complaint wasn't the only one to come to Heather's attention. Every associate had, more than once, asked her what was wrong with their normally cheerful boss.

Heather decided to take action. She didn't appreciate being abruptly spoken to, either. She marched into J.L.'s office, wishing he would leave his cowboy taste at home and decorate with more style. She was actually embarrassed, sometimes, to take people into the room.

Not that J.L. had poor taste, far from it. Growing up in his affluent family, he knew about fine furniture, accessories, and art. J.L.'s home in La Jolla, where the firm's Christmas party was held every year, demonstrated his acute understanding of what was culturally stylish. Heather loved that home. She could see herself as mistress of that home.

Here at the office, though, he stubbornly held to an informal atmosphere. "My clients feel more comfortable sitting on my down-to-earth furniture than they do on that expensive designer sofa we have in the reception room."

"May I speak with you, Mr. Brett?"

"Certainly, Heather."

He did not look up from peering at one of four volumes of *California Reports* that were sprawled, opened, over his mammoth oak desk, near a half-dozen sheets of yellow legal paper showing his illegible handwriting.

"Are you working on your Lucky Dollar case?" she asked.

He gave her such a scowl, she actually took a step backward, amazed that her no-nonsense boss, who was always the epitome of coolness under pressure, had been changed by this case, or this woman, into an emotional inferno.

"I…uh…have something…uh…difficult to say," she began her mission.

"Yes?" J.L. whirled his chair around and grabbed a book that said *American Jurisprudence II* from the shelf. He rifled quickly through the pages, found what he wanted in thirty seconds, and rapidly added it to his notes.

"People are beginning to notice, sir," Heather said.

"Notice what?"

"Your behavior."

He paused and gazed up at her with a squint. "What about my behavior?"

"It's…it's unusual."

"Unusual?"

"Testy."

His eyebrows raised. "Someone's told you this?"

"Several someones."

"Told you I'm testy?"

"And moody, and distracted, and…and, not nice to be around," she concluded bravely.

"I see. Well, that's too bad." J.L. lowered his eyes and began flipping through his notes, but then the full meaning of Heather's words struck him—he was behaving badly toward his employees, something he abhorred, especially since it wasn't their fault.

He knew he owed Heather and the others an apology for being a jerk these days, and he also knew why he was acting that way—it was because of one feisty little blond who had more temper than good sense, more stubbornness than flexibility, and more ways to turn his stomach into knots than he thought any woman could.

Her whirlwind visit to his office had clarified an error in his judgment—he should never have kissed her…held her. It had been unethical to do so because they were on opposite sides of a legal battle. He certainly hadn't planned to do so, but there was just something about Lindsey Faraday that drew him to her every time they were together.

Her accusations to him, that he was using her feelings to advance the case of his client, had hurt deeply. Of course, she was wrong in thinking that, but once he had cooled down, after she had left his office, he had understood how she could have come to that conclusion.

All right. Can't I think the same thing? After all, she didn't pull away from me. She kissed me in return, looked at me with a warm, accepting expression. Couldn't she have been hoping I would convince my client to drop the case once I became involved with her? So, she owes me an apology.

Also, she conveniently forgot that he had given her more

than the allotted time to bring him hard evidence that the loan had been repaid. Didn't she appreciate that? He had had no choice but to file a Notice of Default. Her racing into his office, upsetting his receptionist and secretary, had been uncalled for.

He stood up so suddenly one of his hands overturned a pencil cup on his desk and pens and pencils skittered across papers and onto the floor. Heather gaped at him, and he recognized her disappointment in him.

"Heather, I'm very sorry for my conduct of late. I will do better, I promise, with you and the others." He gave her his best smile but inside, the guilt he felt over making others suffer for his own misconduct raked his conscience.

I need to see Lindsey Faraday, he decided, then just as quickly decided he should stay away from her...far, far away. *Let the law take its course, then I'll deal with the intriguing owner of the Lucky Dollar, and how we feel about each other.*

As though his thoughts had produced her, there was a knock on the open door of his office and both he and Heather looked over to see Lindsey standing there. She was wearing a simple cotton dress, rosy pink in color, with short sleeves and a skirt that brushed the tops of her knees, and J.L. wished at that moment that he were an artist so he could capture her loveliness on canvas.

"No one was at your secretary's desk," she said haltingly, "and I need to see you, J.L."

Quickly, he walked over to her. "Yes, of course, come in." He wondered what was in the box she carried in her arms. "Would you like some coffee? Or tea?"

"Tea would be nice."

As Heather started out the door to accomplish a task she did not welcome, Lindsey laid a hand on her arm. "Heather, I'm sorry about the last time I was here. I know I was rude to you. I hope you'll forgive me."

Heather, surprised at the apology, hastily mumbled, "I suppose so."

"Good." Lindsey gave her a smile. "I assume you got my note."

"Well, uh...."

"Note?" J.L. asked, puzzled.

"Miss Faraday wrote me an apology," Heather explained.

"I see." His attention stayed on his secretary a moment as he wondered why he hadn't been told this, then he turned to Lindsey. "Why don't we sit down and you can tell me why you've come." He directed her to a conversation area near a window where she sat down on a burgundy and hunter green upholstered chair and he seated himself on a matching couch to the side of her.

The fact that Lindsey was here, seated only a few feet from him, made his throat dry, and his breathing quickened as the sun, shining through the window beside her, fell over her long, straight hair hanging down her back, giving it the appearance of spun gold.

It hadn't been easy staying away from her these past many weeks. He had thought of her often and even though she had behaved badly the last time she had been here, she was still a woman he respected and admired, and a vigorous male attraction tempted him to forget his own advice about not pursuing her until their legal differences were settled.

"I can't stay long," she said, looking into his eyes at the same time she extended the box to him.

"What's this?" he asked.

"A replacement for the vase I broke."

J.L. gulped. His vase had cost fifteen hundred dollars. He hoped Lindsey had not spent that. He wouldn't accept it if she had.

Slowly he opened the box and took out a piece of porcelain that amazingly resembled what had been broken, but even a quick look told him it was not worth a tenth of what his had been.

"I know it's not as good as yours," she said, leaning forward, her fingers touching the side of the vase and accidentally brushing his, "but I had to bring you something."

"No, you didn't," he said gently.

"Yes, I did," she insisted. "I behaved abominably."

"You were upset."

"An understatement of fact."

"I should have notified you that I was filing the Notice of Default."

"I knew it was coming. Just not when." Her gaze drifted to the green wool carpet.

He leaned toward her. "That wasn't the whole problem, though. You thought my kissing you was only a ruse to get what my client is asking for."

Slowly Lindsey looked up and her eyes met his, questioning, shimmering blue and moist, and J.L. had to tense every muscle in his body to keep from drawing her into his arms and telling her she was special to him, very special.

"Yes, that's what I thought."

He took a deep breath and let it out slowly, wanting to touch her, hold her hand, convince her his feelings for her were genuine, but he couldn't, not yet.

"Lindsey, let me be honest with you," he said. His voice was soft. "I'm attracted to you…a lot. I have been, since day one when I met you. But we're on opposite sides of an unfortunate situation and, until that is settled, it isn't ethical for us to have a relationship."

"I understand."

"Do you?"

"Yes, because I'm battling the same inconsistency with my own feelings. There are things about you that I like, but then you're threatening my livelihood and those of people I care about. It's hard to separate the two men and, to tell the truth, I can't right now. Anyway, there's another man in my life. He's asked me to marry him."

Heather entered the room with the tea and heard the last words of Lindsey. *J.L. kissed her passionately, but there's another man who wants to marry her?* she thought, incredulous. *What do they see in her, anyway?*

She set the tea things down with a little thump and whirled around, leaving the office. More than ever, she disliked Lindsey Faraday and the power she had over men's feelings.

J.L. struggled with his own feelings, having just heard that there was an important man in Lindsey's life. He hadn't expected that, not the way she had kissed him. How could she care for someone else when he knew, well, was pretty certain, that she had feelings for him? He hoped she wasn't using him the way she had accused him of using her—to get her own way in this legal mess.

"So, there's someone else," he stated, hoping she would give him details.

"Yes, but I didn't come here to talk about him. I came to apologize for my behavior and to ask if it's too late to stop the sale of the mine? I mean, would your client accept monthly payments instead of a lump sum?"

The expression on Lindsey's face was so hopeful, bordering on desperation, that J.L. saw the truth of the situation and sucked in his breath, feeling like he had just been kicked by the meanest bull this side of the Rio Grande.

"You can't pay the thirty thousand, can you?" he asked her.

"I didn't say that."

"All right, then the answer to your question is no. My client needs the money as soon as possible. All of it."

"But wouldn't a monthly amount be better than waiting three months to sell the mine, then going through an escrow period of who-knows-how-long, not to mention the risk of it falling out of escrow and causing even more delays?"

"You need to pay the entire amount, Lindsey."

She stared at him a moment, then rose to her feet. "I see. Well, let me assure you that if, indeed, this is a legitimate claim, then the money will be repaid…somehow…whatever it takes."

He stood up, too, and couldn't help reaching out to take her arm. "Lindsey, can you pay the money?"

She moved away from him, breaking the contact, and walked toward the door. He moved quickly to get in front of her. "Lindsey, tell me. Do you have the thirty thousand dollars to pay my client?"

She looked directly into his eyes. "No, I don't. I have no assets to sell. Every piece of equipment I own is used to mine the Lucky Dollar. There! Are you satisfied? Go back to your barracuda client and tell her she's won." The air sizzled with her frustration.

"Why didn't you tell me this the first day I came to you?" J.L. asked sharply.

"Because I never thought I would have to pay it. But I will. As I said—whatever it takes!"

She pushed around him and walked stiffly out of the office and J.L. watched her go and felt a part of him go with her. Deep anguish ran through him that he, and his client, were pushing Lindsey to the wall, and she most likely would lose the mine that, he knew well enough by now, meant the world to her.

Closing his office door before an interested Heather could ask him any questions, J.L. began pacing. He was angry, with Lindsey's father for not having paid back the money, and with the system of justice that demands reparation even if it means punishing a law-abiding, hard-working person who just happens to be taking the brunt for someone else's mistakes. He wondered if Lindsey's great loyalty to her father would waver now.

For the first time in his successful law career, he was torn between the two sides. He believed in the rights of his client, no doubt about that, but he also felt sick inside that Lindsey was going to suffer because of those rights. He was legally bound to do all he could to bring about a positive resolution for his client, but in the process, he would be destroying Lindsey Faraday, in the name of justice.

Finally settling down at his desk, he glanced over at the coffee table and saw the teacups sitting there, the liquid now cold and untouched. He, though, was not untouched. Every fiber of his being was touched by the predicament of this woman he had just met, and he wanted desperately to help her...but how?

Slumping in his chair, he thought of Lindsey a long time until an idea formed in his head. Then, sitting up straight, he grabbed the phone and dialed a number written on a legal pad in front of him. It was the home number of Santiago Ramirez.

"Mrs. Ramirez? This is J.L. Brett. Is Santiago there? I see. Could you have him call me as soon as he comes in, please? It's important that I talk with him before I go out of town on business. Let me give you my numbers at home and in the car, as well. Thanks a lot. I look forward to meeting you, too."

He put down the phone, and smiled. He felt better. He was going to help Lindsey.

sixteen

"I wish you'd forget about my birthday party," Santiago said
with sincerity when he found Lindsey making out a grocery
list late one afternoon at her desk in the office.

Lindsey looked up, tired. For the past week, in anticipation
of potential buyers looking over the place, she had driven herself and the men relentlessly to complete projects she had let
go for too long. Even so, there was no way she would deprive
Santiago of his party.

She gave him one of her thousand-dollar smiles. "What
would my employees and their families think if I cancelled
one of the Lucky Dollar's oldest traditions? Not to mention
the fact that they'd miss tasting my marvelous chili."

Santiago chuckled. "You don't like to cook."

"But my chili recipe is prize-winning good. Yes?"

"Yes, but with so much on your mind, I hate to see you go to
a lot of trouble just for me. Remember last year what the
Mahoney baby did to your best chair?"

"I remember, and this time I'll be prepared with disposable
diapers in three sizes."

They both laughed and Lindsey stood up. "Santiago, this
may be the last party I'll have for you here at the mine." Her
voice quivered. "Don't deny me this very small way of saying
thank you for all you've meant to my father and me through
the years."

Lindsey saw moisture well up in Santiago's eyes, and quickly
turned away so he wouldn't know she had seen. His emotion
was her emotion. She would miss him terribly. "Besides," she
sighed, "we need a party around here to lighten our spirits. I

know you're as down about selling the mine as I am."

"But we still have some time before that happens. Maybe God will send a miracle and you'll find the money."

Lindsey smiled. "I believe in miracles, Santiago, I really do, but I'm not just sitting back waiting for one to deliver us. Every minute I'm thinking of where I can find that thirty thousand."

"You don't know anyone who could loan it to you?"

"Afraid not."

She came around the desk and gave him a shove toward the front door. "In the meantime, sir, you go home and relax and get ready for your party tomorrow. There's going to be good food, good friends, and good music, and if that doesn't take our minds off our troubles, I don't know what will. Off with you now," she ordered, pushing his bulky body out the door. "I have a party to get ready for."

Santiago obeyed, a grin on his face.

≥♣

The next morning, Lindsey dragged herself out of bed, woefully lacking the energy she needed for the coming day. She had to buy groceries, clean her house, and then cook chili and prepare other food for an onslaught of twenty-two adults and wiggling children who would be invading her home and yard at one o'clock for Santiago's party.

She was tired before she even started—tired in mind as well as body. Giving this party for Santiago, probably the last one, was breaking her heart. Then there was the mine. She had never worked so hard as she had this past week to get the Lucky Dollar in prime condition *if* that terrible day came when she had to sell it. At least if she could get top dollar for it, she could give her well-deserving employees severance pay to ease their disappointment.

Sleepily easing herself into a blue cotton top, well-worn shorts, and floppy sandals, she made a quick trip to the grocery store. Then, back in her kitchen, she became annoyed when a hard knock on her front door interrupted her unpacking of the hamburger, spanish onions, chili beans, and assorted spices she had purchased. She hoped it wasn't one of her employees' wives, coming to graciously offer to help. She wanted to do this party all by herself this time, this last time for Santiago.

She opened the door.

"Hi. I'm here to cook the chili for you."

It was J.L. Brett.

Before Lindsey could stop him, he walked in, with a large grocery bag in one arm and a comment: "I heard cooking is not your forte and, since it's mine, I'll take over."

"I beg your pardon?" Lindsey questioned, wondering who could have betrayed her by telling him that secret. "Thanks, but no thanks. Goodbye."

He didn't get the message, however, and kept right on walking, through her living room, into the kitchen.

She ran behind him, through her house, having to admire his straight back encased in an olive green, short-sleeved shirt and his narrow hips and long, well-built legs clothed in olive green walking shorts.

With his intimidating height and powerful carriage, he would look impressive, striding down the center aisle of a magnificent cathedral, wearing ministerial robes, she thought. Or across the south lawn of the White House, followed by news-hungry reporters. Or along the deck of a battle cruiser, shouting, "Fire the torpedoes!"

Wherever his feet touched, it was territory claimed.

But not in her house!

"Why are you really here?" she yelled at his back, and almost ran into him when he stopped abruptly, without warning.

"I had to see you."

"Your client has died?"

He turned around and scowled at her. "That's not funny."

Crossing her arms over her chest, she gave him a firm look. "I don't think it's funny, either, for you to force your way into my house and disturb my plans for the day."

He flashed her a smile that would melt the sphinx. "I didn't force myself in, you opened the door, and I'm not disturbing, I'm helping."

"I don't need your help."

"Of course you do." He began to remove bottles and packages from the brown bag and plunked them down on the kitchen counters beside Lindsey's supplies. "I didn't bring hamburger. I assumed you had it."

"Of course I have it. But—"

"Great. Let's see. Here's the chili beans, Tabasco, tomato sauce, spanish onions, the chili bricks, chili powder...I put one tablespoon of chili powder per pound, in my basic recipe."

"One tablespoon?" Lindsey gasped. "I use only one teaspoon."

"Oh, good chili needs more." His look was recriminating. "Gives it a real bite."

"That's too hot for my taste."

"Hot is good."

"Not for me."

He grinned. "How do you know till you've tried it?"

Lindsey's blood began to boil. "I don't need your advice on how to make chili," she said sharply, "and what makes you think I'm cooking up a batch today, anyway?"

"Because Santiago's birthday party is this afternoon, right?" He began to rummage through the drawers for utensils.

"Yes," she conceded, "but you're not invited."

"Santiago said I could come."

"He did not."

"Did, too. And not only did he invite me," J.L. went on in a disgustingly cheerful banter, pulling out a wooden spoon, a spatula, and a six-inch-long knife that he laid on the counter beside the sack, "he said I would be welcome."

"What?"

"I guess he was speaking for himself and not the hostess."

"Most definitely."

Lindsey was almost in shock. Why would Santiago invite this man to the party when he knew how she felt about J.L. Brett and this horrible legal situation?

"Before you decide to fire the man," J.L. said, washing his hands in the sink, "you should know that the main reason he invited me was so that I could talk to one of your men who works at the mine."

"About whether or not I properly pay him and provide adequate health insurance?"

J.L. chuckled. "No. It's a family matter."

"Santiago thinks you can advise him?"

"Yep. More comfortably here at the party than in my office."

That conclusion made sense, but Lindsey was still thoroughly puzzled why her devoted foreman was suddenly so chummy with the "enemy" and she mutely watched J.L. whip open the door beneath the sink, find the paper towels, and wipe his wet hands. Then he faced her. "Do you have an apron?"

Lindsey's eyes bugged wide. "Now just one minute," and she grabbed his left arm as he started opening one drawer after another in search of the garment.

Her reaction to touching his skin, to feeling the strong mat of hair that covered his forearm, jolted her. It was like touching fire that then raced through her body, leaving her limp. From simply touching him. She was in trouble.

She dropped her hand as though scalded. "I cannot keep you from attending Santiago's party since he invited you himself, but I do not want or need your help. Please leave my house."

Ignoring her tirade, J.L. searched until he found the drawer that held aprons and potholders. From it he took a well-used white terry cloth apron with a deer on the front, tied it around his waist, and said, "This will do, don't you think?"

Lindsey refused to smile, even though the rugged hunk of a man before her looked deceptively domesticated, and docile, which were definitely two words she would never use to describe him.

"You're a regular Betty Crocker," she declared, then glanced at her watch. "When you came in, you said you had to see me. Are you wanting to remind me that the ninety-day deadline's almost up, then the mine will be sold and you'll be victorious?"

J.L. frowned and shook his head no. "Lindsey, I'm not insensitive to what you're going through."

"Really? You're giving a good imitation."

"I've been more than lenient with the time I've given you to prove the loan was repaid."

"That's true." She was going to say more, but she felt tears spring into her eyes, and turned her back on him, not wanting him to see her emotion. Her nerves were frazzled these days, and every time she thought of losing the mine, she got either mad or sad.

She felt him come up behind her, close. "Talk to me, Lindsey," he pleaded, his voice low and gentle beside her ear.

She didn't want to talk with him. She wanted him out of her house, out of her life.

"Have you found any way to raise the money you need?" he asked.

"No, but I'm not giving up. We're mining every day. I can hope—"

"You've tried the banks?"

"Of course."

"Relatives with money?"

"There's no one."

"Friends?" Instantly she thought of Lance, and just as quickly dismissed the thought. She had too much pride to ask him for money. Besides, if he gave it to her, she would feel more than obligated to marry him, and she was pretty sure Lance was not the right man for her.

"I...don't think so," she answered J.L.'s question. In ultimate frustration, she said, "So, file your notices in the newspapers, Mr. Brett. Put up a 'For Sale' sign on my property. Sell...." Her voice broke. "Sell the Lucky Dollar."

He moved toward her, but she put up her hands to keep him at a distance. "I know what you're thinking, that I'm silly about the mine. After all, it's just a piece of property, a thing, a possession. But to me, the Lucky Dollar is the embodiment of my life with my father, the days and months and years I spent with him growing up, learning the business, having him proud of me, being loved by him unconditionally. How can I give that up?"

With a gentle touch, he reached out and pulled her into his arms, and while she at first resisted, it was infinitely easier to give in and let her face rest on his broad chest while the tears she could not prevent rushed down her cheeks.

seventeen

Silent moments passed and Lindsey grew content in J.L.'s arms, for they circled her like a safe haven that would protect her from anything bad happening to her. Of course the idea was ludicrous since it was J.L. himself, representing some nameless client, who was taking away her peace.

She pulled away from him and looked around the kitchen—anywhere other than into his eyes that she suspected would be filled with concern and would melt her heart.

"I'm going to be fine," she assured him with more pluck than she actually possessed at that moment.

"Good girl." He lifted her face with one of his hands and gazed at her. "I care about what happens to you, Lindsey. Can you believe that?"

Lindsey's pulse raced and she tried to answer as steadily as possible, "I'm not sure, J.L."

"Please try."

She gave him a tiny smile. "I will."

"Great, because believe it or not, I don't want to see the mine sold away from you any more than you do. I know how much it means to you."

Lindsey wanted to believe him. It would be so comforting to do so. His sentiment seemed sincere, but could she trust him? After all, she could not forget that he had kissed her intensely, at the mine, and still had filed a Notice of Default against her.

"It might be that God has a better plan for your life than running the mine," J.L. suggested. "Have you thought about that?"

"My pastor brought up the same idea last Sunday," she told

him honestly, "but I'm resisting it."

J.L. squeezed her arms, then let her go and turned toward the living room. "Did I see a Bible on one of your tables?" he asked.

"Yes. Why?"

"There's an obscure couple of verses in the Old Testament, written by the prophet Jeremiah, that fit your situation perfectly."

He walked briskly out of the kitchen and into the living room where he found her Bible, whipped skillfully through the pages, then handed it back to Lindsey.

"Jeremiah 29, eleven to thirteen," he said.

Hesitantly, she took the sacred book from him, surprised at his familiarity with it. Slowly, her eyes lowered from his face to the white pages before her.

"Why not read the verses out loud?" he prodded, and when Lindsey found the reference, she did just that, in a quiet manner, still in awe that the very words of God were available to her, and everyone, to read and inspire.

" 'For I know the thoughts that I think toward you, saith the Lord, thoughts of peace, and not of evil, to give you an expected end. Then shall ye call upon me, and ye shall go and pray unto me, and I will harken unto you. And ye shall seek me, and find me, when ye shall search for me with all your heart.' "

Lindsey looked into J.L. eyes, as the tremendous impact of those words settled in her brain. "Do you really believe that, J.L., that God cares so much about each one of us?" she whispered.

J.L. nodded yes. "His promises are everlasting, Lindsey, and He is faithful in keeping those promises."

"How do you know that?"

"Because it's happened in my life. I'll tell you about it someday."

How could Lindsey argue with that? J.L. seemed to have strong faith, just as she hoped to have, and a thorough knowledge of the Bible. Was it that knowledge that gave him his confidence in God's faithfulness?

She closed the book, laid it down, and walked back into the kitchen, her heart suddenly stabbed with the realization that she had always thought her father was faithful to his promises, too. He had told her the mine would be her inheritance forever...forever. For her and her children and grandchildren. His promise was about to be broken. How could J.L. be so sure that God would not also break a promise?

"Thank you for showing me that," she said to J.L. when he joined her in the kitchen. "I'll...think about it."

"You won't be sorry to put your trust in the Lord, Lindsey."

"We'll see," she countered, a stubborn part of her old nature still not able to totally grasp this new relationship she had with the God of the universe. "For now, you'll have to excuse me. I have lots of chili to make, and other tasks to complete before Santiago's party."

"I'll help."

Before she could stop him, J.L. went to the refrigerator and took from it six pounds of hamburger meat and put them next to the stove.

"J.L., I really don't need your help."

He stopped unwrapping the meat and clucked his tongue. "You know, lady, the first day I met you I put down on my list that you were uncooperative. You were then, and you still are."

Lindsey garroted him with a look of unbelief. "You have a list on me? That says I'm uncooperative?" She picked up one of the spanish onions and gripped it fiercely. "How else do you describe me?"

"Stubborn. Temperamental. Defensive. Unrealistic."

"Oooooo." Her howl resounded through the tiny kitchen

and she raised her hand to throw the onion, but J.L. snatched the vegetable from her hand and tossed it into the sink.

"I added loyal and compassionate to it."

"Wonderful."

"And I'm sure I put down beautiful. And intriguing."

"Oh."

"And intoxicating."

"Really?"

"As well as stunning and intelligent."

"My, my."

With a move that caught her off guard, J.L. reached out for Lindsey and pulled her against him, lowering his mouth until his lips hovered tantalizingly over hers.

"In other words, Lindsey Faraday, you're not like any other woman I've ever known,"

Then he kissed her, intently, his arms sliding around her waist in an eager possessiveness that sent Lindsey's senses exploding into awareness, heightened by the salty taste of his hungry lips on hers, the scent of his cologne, and the feel of his muscled arms as she clutched them for support.

"J.L., we can't do this," she whispered, her cheek next to his. "You were the one who said we should wait to start a relationship until this legal problem is solved."

"Yes, I did say that, didn't I?" He kissed the tip of her nose. "And I should take my own counsel." He stroked her cheek. "Why then, do I find it practically impossible to stay away from you?" His look was tender. "But I have to, don't I?"

"Yes."

He straightened, took in a lungful of air, let it out, and released her. "Okay, you're the boss. I think I'll get to work on something less volatile than you," and he put cooking oil in each of the three dutch ovens.

Lindsey eyed him skeptically. "*If* I let you stay and help, do you promise to put in only one teaspoon of chili powder per pound of meat?"

J.L. looked pained. "You don't know what you're missing."

Lindsey laughed out loud. "Yes, I do."

"How about a compromise?" When Lindsey reluctantly agreed, J.L. winked at her, and she sighed. "I'll start on the salad." Gathering together the lettuce, celery, tomatoes, and hard-boiled eggs gave her time to get herself under control, but there was something she had to say, that J.L. had to hear.

She paused from her work and waited until he was looking at her, then she said decisively, "I must be honest with you, J.L. I'm powerfully attracted to you, now, but if the Lucky Dollar is sold, and my employees are out of work, and I end up losing the dream of my life, I'm not sure I'll want to have anything to do with you."

ɜ҉

Forty minutes before the party was due to begin, Lindsey collapsed on the back porch swing, holding a frosty glass of lemonade in her hand, and took a deep breath.

She was ready, amazingly, despite the interruption of J.L. that morning. He had helped her not only with the chili (his recipe was better than hers, she had to admit), but also with setting up the tables and chairs on the lawn. Together they had hung gaily colored balloons on several tree branches and arranged red plastic plates, silverware, and napkins on the red-and-white checkered tablecloths covering the tables. J.L. had even tried on one of the funny hats to be given to the children in attendance, and Lindsey had tried, unsuccessfully, to pin the tail on the paper donkey tacked to an ancient oak tree.

They had made it a point not to talk of anything personal, and the time had passed quickly, and comfortably.

Then she had shooed him away so she could clean the house, which he had offered to do while she showered and changed clothes, but she had declined.

"I do have something I need to buy in town," he had said

then, "but I'll be back soon," and off he had gone.

Thinking about their morning together, Lindsey realized that working with J.L. had been fun. He had been patient, diligent to detail, and had seemed to enjoy getting things ready as much as she had.

Closing her eyes now, hoping for a few more minutes of peace before the onslaught began, Lindsey heard the crunch of gravel as someone came along the path from the front of the house to the back. Thinking that some of her guests were arriving early, she opened her eyes and saw J.L.

"Do the caterers have everything ready?" he joked, the twinkle in his eyes warming her heart.

"Yes, indeedy. They've come and gone, leaving me nothing to do."

"Except talk to your first guest. Me."

"I can handle that." But no sooner were the words out of her mouth than Lindsey wondered if she had spoken too soon. J.L., tall and tanned, had changed into brown brushed denims and a forest green western shirt with embroidered circles on the yoke. A snakeskin belt wrapped its way around his trim waist and ended in a matching buckle with his initials on it. Between snakeskin boots and a green paisley Apache tie lying jauntily around his neck, he looked anything but a man to be handled.

Lindsey swallowed hard.

"I'm glad you approve," he said with a wink, coming up to the swing and taking from behind his back the biggest bunch of red tulips she had ever seen in her life.

"Oh, J.L.," she gasped, "they're gorgeous."

"I thought you could put them on the tables. Didn't I see some glass Mason jars in one of your cupboards?"

"Yes, you did. What a perfect idea. Thank you so much."

She smiled warmly at him and sniffed the flowers as he eased himself down on the swing beside her.

"I approve of you, too, Lindsey," he said, the brown of his eyes deepening. "You look…incredible in that blouse," and with two fingers he reached out and carefully felt the material of one billowy, long sleeve that ended in a cuff of ruffles and lace. "You remind me of a cool, delicious dish of mint ice cream."

"Do I?"

Lindsey sat very still as he touched the high, banded-lace collar of the blouse, trimmed with tiny ribbons. When she had bought the blouse, she had wondered if it were too feminine for her. Though it went perfectly with her black dress jeans, it was quite a change from the plain western shirts she usually wore at the mine.

"Can I help you put those flowers into water?" he offered.

"No, I'll be just a minute. Why don't you sit here and enjoy the solitude. There won't be much of that for the next few hours."

J.L. chuckled while Lindsey hurried into the house, willing her heart to stop pounding. But how could it, when she knew J.L.'s eyes were watching every step she took?

eighteen

"I'm sure the party will be a success, Lindsey," J.L. said, when they set the last Mason jar of glorious tulips in the center of the table where Santiago would sit.

"Your chili will help."

"I hope so. I got the recipe from my father."

"Is he a chef?"

"No. Chili is the one and only dish in his entire cookbook." Lindsey smiled. "Tell me about your family."

They went back to the swing and sat down together. J.L. began the swing moving, slowly, and said, "I have a lovely, elegant mother and a somewhat pompous father, both of whom I adore, no brothers or sisters, but a big Labrador I call Brute, and a house in La Jolla."

"Do you get on well with your parents?"

"Pretty much, although more so with my mother."

"Tell me about her."

J.L.'s expression became contemplative, and Lindsey recognized love and respect in his gaze. "She's a special woman, regal but unpretentious, who cares about people, as you do, and won't put up with rudeness or unkindness. She feels she has the right to know about every woman I go out with, and gives me her opinion of them, whether I want it or not."

Lindsey giggled. "She sounds delightful."

"She is, and precious to my father and me."

"What is he like?"

J.L. snorted softly. "Dad is a handsome and charming guy. People like him instantly, which he takes advantage of when he's raising huge amounts of money for charity."

"Does he do that for a living?"

"No. He plays with corporations…buys up small ones, improves management, then sells them for good profit. He thrives on having and making money. It's his *raison d'être*."

"Which you don't approve of?"

"Oh, I wouldn't say that. We just have different goals. I respect my dad, his drive, and sense of fair play. He's a hard man to do business with, but an honest one. He's given me his self-confidence."

Lindsey smiled and offered him some more lemonade from the pitcher she had brought out after arranging the tulips. "Do you get your compassion for people from your mother?"

J.L. thought about that a moment. "Yes, I think I do. You'd like her, Lindsey."

"I'm sure I would."

He shifted on the swing and faced her more directly, his leg sprawled across the seat. "What's your mother like, Lindsey? I've heard you talk about your father, but never her."

Lindsey looked away from him. "That's because she's barely a part of my life."

"Oh?"

"She gave up my father and me to pursue her concert career. I've never understood that. Of course, my father didn't make their life together easy when he gave up his own career as a stockbroker and bought the Lucky Dollar. Mother hated the place on sight, and only came here once. The marriage ended shortly thereafter."

"I'm sorry." J.L. reached out and took her hand. "Have you missed her?"

"I did unbelievably the first year, then it got easier."

"Do you hear from her?"

Lindsey looked off into the distance. "Through the years she's faithfully sent me birthday and Christmas cards with hastily scribbled notes saying she looks forward to seeing me soon, but soon never comes." She shrugged. "I've gotten used to life without her."

J.L. doubted that were true. He couldn't imagine a full life without the presence of his mother, and he was sure a woman as sensitive as Lindsey needed one, too.

"So you and your father came to Majestic."

"Yes, and loved it because the pace was slow and the people were friendly. They didn't care how big our house was or if we were wearing the latest fashion. I loved the mine, too, because I could run through the tunnels, and hold real gold in my hands, and only had to wear a dress on Sundays when we'd go to church."

"I would like to have known your dad," J.L. said somberly.

"Everyone liked him. He was a happy, positive-thinking man—and infinitely patient with me." She tucked one of her feet underneath her and turned to face J.L. "He used to tell me over and over, 'Some day, Pumpkin, you and I are going to find the Mother Lode.'" She gulped back a sudden lump in her throat. "Obviously we didn't find it since your client's relative had to lend him...." She choked on the words.

It was all J.L. could do to keep from reaching out and taking Lindsey in his arms. The war raged inside him, one side saying to hold Lindsey and never let her go, and the other warning him to stay away from her until the legal mess was settled.

He loved holding her, smelling the sweetness of her perfume, touching her skin, nuzzling her shiny hair. He had never had trouble before choosing directions, making tough decisions that needed making, but with Lindsey Faraday, it was tearing him apart to deny his feelings for her that grew stronger every day despite disagreements, harsh words, and even a kick in the shins.

There was so much about her to admire: her intelligence, loyalty to others, compassion, how hard she worked, and a whole lot of other things that added up to one strong but vulnerable woman he wanted in his life, maybe even permanently.

ಸಿ

The party was a roaring success, as was J.L.'s chili, and the man himself. Lindsey could not believe how well he fitted in with everyone.

The men found him unaffected and down-to-earth and genuinely interested in their everyday lives. The women were charmed by his rugged good looks, urbane conversation, and appreciation for their beautiful children. The eight children themselves, ranging in age from four months to fourteen years, found him a willing partner for baby talk or games of ring toss or touch football.

Lindsey didn't chide Santiago for inviting him, for she wanted nothing to spoil this last celebration they would share.

"This is the best party of them all," the guest of honor said, looking very handsome in a startling white, western bib shirt and new black denims. His dark hair was slicked back and the bushy brows above his eyes were wetted down to keep them under control.

"I'm glad you think so," Lindsey responded, "because it's for the best foreman anyone ever had." She gave him a hug, and when he apologized for inviting J.L. without telling her, she told him it was okay.

J.L. walked up to them. "Happy birthday, Santiago."

The two men shook hands vigorously. "Thanks, Señor Brett."

"Call me J.L. Is your friend here? The one you want me to talk with?"

"He's late, but he'll be along. I'll get you when he comes."

"Great."

Santiago walked off and J.L. smiled down at Lindsey, the laugh lines around his eyes telling her he was more used to smiling than frowning. "I'd say your party is a hit."

"It does look that way, doesn't it?"

Maria, Santiago's wife, paused on her way to one of the picnic tables with a tray full of french bread. "Are you two having a good time?" Her eyes skirted from Lindsey to J.L. where they rested long enough to give him homage, not that Lindsey blamed her.

"We're doing great, Mrs. Ramirez," J.L. answered her with one of his melt-women-into-the-ground smiles. "I'm glad you and I got to meet."

"Me, too." Turning to Lindsey she said, "Thank you for this party for Santiago. He is thrilled with it. You are so kind," and she leaned over the tray of bread and kissed Lindsey's cheek.

"Believe me, Maria, it is little enough to do for all that Santiago, and you, have meant to me through the years."

Maria went on her way, delivering the bread to hungry people who were everywhere—in the house, out on the grass, talking, laughing, playing games, and eating all they wanted.

"Nice woman," J.L. summarized.

"The best."

"She thinks you're number one."

"How do you know that?"

"She told me. When does the entertainment start?"

"Wait a minute," Lindsey said, her eyes widening. "What do you mean she told you? When? Where? *Why?*"

"My, my, so many questions," J.L. teased. "Oh, I see some guys setting up now. What do they play?"

"Country western," Lindsey answered distractedly, not wanting to stray from finding out what Maria was up to.

"Darlin', that's my favorite kind." J.L. clapped his hands enthusiastically. "Maybe I can join them."

"What do you mean?"

"I play a pretty good guitar."

"J.L., I don't think so—"

"Don't worry. I'm not shy. I have my instrument in my

truck. I'll go get it and sing a few songs to warm everyone up for the main event." He gave her a wink. "And I won't even charge you." He strode off and Lindsey ground her teeth, realizing that this man was unstoppable once he set his mind to something.

His musical ability surprised her and pleased her guests to no end. He sang a couple of Clint Black and Alan Jackson songs with a clear voice that was easy to listen to and got everyone tapping their feet.

It was unbelievable how he stepped right into the lives of these strangers and had them eating out of his hand. They loved his chili. They loved his music. They loved him.

The question that haunted Lindsey was how to keep herself from loving him, too. If this was the real J.L. Brett, he was everything in a man she could possibly want. But if he were deceiving her for his own purposes, it would be cruel to lose her heart to him as well as her mine.

A small voice chided her for continuing to mistrust J.L., but Lindsey couldn't help it. A lot was at stake here.

She saw the object of her contemplation across the yard, standing with Santiago and Pete Donaldson. J.L. was listening intently to what Pete was saying.

More apprehension fell over Lindsey that Santiago seemed to like the very man who was tearing the Lucky Dollar away from her. Even though she knew J.L. was just doing his job, representing someone with a legitimate claim against the mine, it still felt personal to her, as though he, himself, were the cause of her misfortune. Her temper flared.

Moving toward the house, she said goodbye en route to some of the guests who were leaving. In the kitchen, she found a tray of leftover food on a counter and worked furiously for the next ten minutes putting things away, yanking plastic bowls out of the cupboard for storing the remaining chili and salad, and fiercely tearing food storage bags from their box for the french bread.

"It isn't fair," she muttered angrily. "It just isn't fair."

"What isn't?"

She whirled around to see J.L. standing there, with Santiago beside him. She felt like yelling at them both, but she couldn't, without spoiling Santiago's party, and she could never do that to him.

"All these leftovers," she fibbed, gesturing toward the pile of plastic bags and colored bowls. "I'll be big as a house if I have to eat them all myself."

"But we'll both still love you, won't we, Santiago?" J.L. kidded.

Santiago agreed.

Lindsey heard the word "love" and dismissed it as a figure of speech. There was no way J.L. Brett could love her on the one hand and be destroying her on the other.

Maria came into the room and slipped her hands around her husband's waist. "I knew I'd find you in the kitchen, sneaking more to eat." She turned to J.L. "You make great chili, J.L., but not as good as Lindsey's. It's a little too hot."

They all laughed, especially J.L. and Lindsey when they exchanged a secret look and he winked at her. Then Santiago shook J.L.'s hand and ushered Maria out the door, and Lindsey kept smiling as she heard them go, but wouldn't have been if she had known that Santiago and Maria had decided that J.L. Brett was the perfect man for her.

nineteen

Around five o'clock, after most of the guests had gone, J.L. leaned back against one of the kitchen counters, folded his arms across his chest, and just stared at Lindsey. She was so heart-stopping beautiful, so nice to people, so good and decent and plucky.

The list he had started on her when they had first met now had many words on it to describe her, a few negative ones, but mostly positive words that explained why, this day, his mouth had gone dry every time he had seen her and heard her voice saying encouraging things to the guests.

Just how close am I, he wondered, *to falling in love with her? Or has it already happened? How does one know?*

He saw the frown on her face now, and asked, "What's wrong?"

"Nothing," Lindsey insisted in a high falsetto voice, scooping up used plates and utensils and throwing them into a huge plastic garbage bag. But J.L. could feel the animosity racing across the room from her to him, and wondered what had triggered it.

He watched the muscles in her back tighten up and the way she avoided looking at him. After a few minutes he said, "What happened to the friendship we had this morning, Lindsey?"

"I don't know what you mean."

"Yes, you do. Tell me the truth, please."

Lindsey raised her head and looked him straight in the eye, "I'm trying, J.L., I really am, to be civilized over the fact that in a short time my life will be turned upside down...by you."

"This is not a personal fight between us, Lindsey."

"It feels like it."

"You're making it that way."

"I know, and you're just doing your job, but you've intruded yourself into my life and I feel like everything is slipping out of my control. The mine is going. You have Santiago, as well as Maria, eating out of your hand, and all my employees and their families think you're Mr. Wonderful."

"But you don't."

She lowered her eyes and went back to her cleanup work, knowing she could not answer that question to his face, and not wanting him to see how really upset she was. She felt like that mountain lion she had shot at in the mine. He wanted all other lions to know this was his territory. Well, she had territory, too, and J.L. had invaded it, conquered it, and, worst of all, was well on the way to conquering her, too.

She understood why her friends and employees thought he was terrific. She did, too.

As the party had progressed, she had been aware of a growing resentment toward J.L., and how easily he fit in with the people she loved. Of course, none of them knew what was about to happen to the mine, but that didn't alter her sense of betrayal, that "her" people were slipping over to the enemy camp and she was being left alone to struggle against the encroaching danger.

"I can't be a good sport about losing my mine," she said, "especially since I don't feel the claim against it is valid."

"Lindsey, you've seen the evidence."

She heard the censure in his voice and it was like a twig snapping in her spirit. Try as she would, she couldn't prevent the law from taking from her what she didn't want to give. She could kick, scream, and protest all she wanted, but J.L. Brett had the upper hand.

"Fine," she snapped. "Sell the mine. Fire my employees. Laugh all the way to the bank with your—"

"That does it!" J.L. roared, interrupting her tirade. Reaching out, he grabbed her hand and yanked her toward the door. Plastic dinnerware flew to the floor as he announced, "It's time you learned the truth."

"About what?" Lindsey struggled to be free of him, but her effort was useless.

"About who is going to get the thirty thousand dollars."

"I know who—your client!"

"You need to understand the circumstances."

They were outside now and he was pulling her along the path toward his truck.

"J.L., let me go. I have to clean up from the party."

"Later."

Lindsey saw that Santiago and Maria hadn't left the property yet, but were quietly talking with some folks beside a rose hedge. They looked up when they heard Lindsey and J.L. coming.

"Let go of me," Lindsey ordered between gritted teeth.

"If you behave yourself and come with me without fuss, I will."

"All right," she promised, but the minute he let go of her, she turned on her heels and started back for the house.

"Hey, come back here," he yelled, then charged after her.

"I have work to do, Mr. Lawyer."

"That's the trouble with you, Miss Faraday—you don't think of anything but work. Well, it's time you saw that there are other things in life more important."

"Such as?"

"You'll see."

"I'm not going anywhere with you, J.L. Brett." Lindsey dug the heels of her boots into the soft earth and clamped her arms across her chest in determination.

J.L. scooped her off the ground and dumped her over his shoulder.

"Put me down!" she shrieked. "What do you think you're

doing?"

"You're going to meet my client, Lindsey girl," came the determined answer as J.L.'s lengthy strides took them past a gaping Santiago and Maria and friends.

"I am not going anywhere with you!" Lindsey squirmed as much as she could, beating her hands against his back while her head bobbed up and down.

"Yes, you are."

Lindsey could not believe how fast he moved despite her fighting him with all her strength. "Santiago! Maria!" she screamed for help, but neither of them tried to stop J.L. *They'll answer for this,* Lindsey vowed, especially when she saw a smile on Maria's face.

They were almost to J.L.'s truck when she heard a familiar voice.

"Lindsey!"

She gasped, and squirmed around over J.L.'s shoulder just enough to see Lance staring at her, incredulous.

"What's going on here?" he demanded to know.

"I'm kidnapping Miss Faraday," J.L. answered roughly. "Excuse us, please," and he strode around Lance whose mouth dropped open.

"Help me, Lance," Lindsey pleaded, stretching her arms out toward him. They were at the truck now.

Maria and Santiago hurried up to them, staring at the scene she and J.L. were making. She felt like the star attraction in a grade B movie. It was degrading.

"Put her down," Lance told J.L. "Right now." The words were more a plea than an order, Lindsey noticed with a sinking heart. Lance was no match for J.L.

"Exactly my plan," J.L. declared, bending powerful thighs so he could open the passenger door. "The party's over," he said to Lance, "if that's why you've come."

"It isn't. I'm here to see my fiancèe."

J.L.'s body went rigid and Lindsey heard a slight intake of

his breath just before he unceremoniously slid her off his shoulder, but held onto her arm.

"Your fiancèe?" With raised eyebrows, he turned to face Lindsey.

Before she could disclaim Lance's rash statement, he stepped closer to J.L. and said firmly, "Who are you, and what do you want with Lindsey?" His eyes narrowed and Lindsey thought he might actually be bold enough to challenge J.L. but, before a confrontation between the two men arose, she said, "Lance, this is J.L. Brett. He's an attorney and—"

"J.L. Brett? Of Brett and Associates, and the San Diego Bretts?" The light that sprang into his eyes and the transformation in his face from concern to awe puzzled Lindsey.

"One and the same," J.L. answered him, releasing Lindsey's arm and extending his hand to Lance. "Your name, sir?"

"Lance Robards."

"Robards, Robards." J.L. tried to recall the name.

"I own the Trivoli restaurants, in La Jolla as well as San Diego." Lance stuck out his chest in pride. "You may have dined at one of them."

"Can't say that I have."

"Heard of them, at least."

"Sorry."

Lance's crestfallen look almost made Lindsey laugh, but he quickly recovered. "Then you must come for dinner one night, as my guest."

J.L. smiled as Lindsey frowned over Lance's fawning. Why did he think J.L. Brett was such a big deal?

"I'd be happy to…uh, Lance was it?"

"Yes. Lance Robards. R-o-b-a-r-d-s."

"I'll remember."

"Perhaps tonight?" Lance suggested, looking at the expensive watch on his wrist. "We could all go together. I'm sure you'd find something you'd like on our sophisticated menu. I have extraordinary chefs."

J.L. shook his head. "Sorry, can't. Miss Faraday and I have some business to take care of."

"Now?"

Lindsey moved away from J.L. and slipped her arm through Lance's, a move that brought an immediate rise to Lance's shoulders. "Lance, Mr. Brett is attorney for the party claiming the Lucky Dollar owes her thirty thousand dollars."

Lance's eyebrows rose. "I see."

"He thinks I need to meet the person…tonight."

"Tonight?"

"Right now, as a matter of fact," J.L. jumped in, giving Lance a manly slap on the back. "So, if you'll excuse us, Robards, we'll be going."

"We're not going anywhere," Lindsey insisted.

"You need to meet her, Lindsey. It will make you feel better."

"Ha! How could anything make me feel good about giving up thirty thousand dollars or selling my mine?"

"Trust me." J.L. gestured with his hand, palm up, toward the passenger door, as though he were directing her into a golden chariot.

Lindsey hesitated.

"Maybe you should go, sweetheart," Lance suggested, his eyes dashing from Lindsey to J.L. then back to Lindsey. "I'll come back tomorrow night, and we'll…talk."

"Go ahead, boss," Santiago said. "We'll warm up some chili for Mr. Robards so he won't have driven all this way for nothing."

"Good idea, Santiago," J.L. exclaimed, gently taking Lindsey's hand and leading her to the door of the truck. "Do you like your chili hot, Robards?"

Lance grimaced. "Certainly not."

J.L. chuckled in Lindsey's ear. "Figures."

She gave him a scowl and got into the truck.

twenty

"I didn't know you were engaged," J.L. said sharply to Lindsey as they drove into San Diego.

"And I didn't know your family was prominent society."

"Have you set a wedding date?"

"Now I understand why, since you were born with the proverbial silver spoon in your mouth, it's easy for you to ask me to pay your client thirty thousand dollars. Just like that."

"You told me you were attracted to me."

"Since you've never had to scrounge for money—"

"Could we talk about the same thing, please? How serious are you and Lance Robards?"

"I don't want to talk about it."

"Great. Are you going to marry him so you can get the money to save the mine?"

Lindsey gasped. "How can you think I would marry a man I don't love just to get my hands on his money—"

"Aha, so you don't love him."

"I didn't say that."

"Yes, you did."

The smile on J.L.'s face was so maddening that Lindsey wanted to slap it off.

"I'll bet you're not even engaged."

When she refused to answer him, he went on. "Robards probably just said that to let me know you were off limits, like the mountain lions do when they leave scrapes to define their territory."

"Oh, please, I'm not a piece of property to be fought over."

"No, you're not. Are you going to marry him?"

Lindsey clasped her hands together until they turned white and then stared straight ahead. Why should she answer such a personal question? Actually she couldn't answer it. She didn't know herself.

"He's not right for you," J.L. informed her.

She jerked her head to stare at him. "You don't even know him."

"I've met men like him. They're interested only in themselves."

"Really?"

"Does he approve of you owning and running the Lucky Dollar?"

"No comment."

"I'll bet he wants you to give it up if you get married."

"No comment."

J.L. began to whistle. "No comment necessary, m'lady. Lance Robards is a nerd and you're too smart to marry him."

Lindsey ground her teeth and stared at the floor, praying they would reach their destination before she strangled Mr. Know-It-All Brett.

"My client's name is Mindy Carson," he said as he turned the truck into a poor neighborhood where houses were run-down and the grass, if there was any, was brown and patchy. The words were the first ones spoken by either of them for ten minutes. "She's very nice. You'll like her."

Lindsey groaned. "I will like the person who is going to take my mine away from me? You're out of your mind."

J.L. chuckled softly and said, "We'll see."

Lindsey turned away from him in the seat and stared out at the rundown neighborhood. She couldn't get over Lance's deference to J.L. Quickly enough he had forgotten her being forced against her will to go with J.L. and shamelessly had begged the wealthy, influential man to patronize his restaurants. She had been embarrassed for Lance who hadn't the common sense to be embarrassed for himself.

She also felt uncomfortable with J.L. thinking she was engaged to Lance when it was neither officially true nor likely to be. The more she was with J.L., the more she realized her feelings for Lance were not strong enough for marriage. But J.L. was just so sure of himself, he needed a blow to his ego to bring him in line. She wished she hadn't slipped and intimated she didn't love Lance. She was fond of him, after all.

The truck stopped in front of a tiny, yellow stucco house whose sidewalk was cracked and where two lonely daffodils sat in a dry patch of ground that at one time had been a garden before the weeds had taken over.

"We're here," J.L. announced.

Lindsey already understood one powerful reason why Mindy Carson wanted her money, and wanted it all—to find a better neighborhood in which to live. This one was depressing. It even looked dangerous.

"Maybe she isn't home," Lindsey said.

"She probably is. She doesn't go out much."

He opened the truck door for Lindsey to get out and together they walked up to the rickety wooden porch badly in need of a paint job. As they came to the front door, Lindsey brushed a cobweb from her arm and J.L. knocked.

"Who is it?" came a female voice from inside.

"J.L. Brett, Miss Carson. May I see you?"

"Of course. Give me a minute."

They waited and heard a lock on the other side of the door being fumbled with. Finally the voice called out, "Please come in."

J.L. opened the door for Lindsey, and the two of them stepped into a narrow and dark hallway with fading flowered wallpaper and plain brown linoleum on the floor.

At the end of the hallway was a young woman, very pretty, with light brown hair softly framing a round, pale face—and sitting in a wheelchair.

Her frail body looked almost like a child's in its simple shirt-waist dress, and her eyes looked tired even though there was a lovely expression on her face that showed no irritation at being interrupted from her evening's activity.

"This is a surprise visit, Mr. Brett," she said.

"Yes, Miss Carson. I'm sorry for the time, and that I didn't call first, but it was a last-minute decision to come."

"That's perfectly all right. Let's go into the living room where there's more light and you can introduce me to your friend."

Lindsey's mind was whirling. *Surely this can't be the woman who wants my money?* Immediate compassion rushed out to her as Lindsey wondered why she was incapacitated.

Mindy Carson expertly turned her chair around and moved it into another room, and Lindsey and J.L. followed.

The small but immaculate living room was filled with soft light and old furniture, but not much of it for space was needed to accommodate the wheelchair.

"Miss Carson, I'd like to introduce you to Lindsey Faraday, the owner of the Lucky Dollar." J.L. turned his gaze to Lindsey. "Mindy is the client I represent," he said softly. "It was her mother who loaned your father the money."

"I see," Lindsey said softly.

Mindy exclaimed, "How nice to meet you, Miss Faraday." With a genuine smile enhanced by lovely white teeth, she extended her hands, which Lindsey awkwardly took, feeling suddenly uncomfortable at being here with the woman about whom she had thought unkindly. Mindy's eyes brightened. "It must be exciting to have a gold mine," she assumed.

Lindsey glanced at J.L. before smiling weakly at Mindy and saying, "It is. I love it. One never knows what the ground is going to give up from day to day."

Mindy nodded enthusiastically. "Maybe someday I can come

and take a tour of it. Could I get my wheelchair through the tunnels?"

"On the main level, yes," Lindsey answered as calmly as she could, knowing there weren't many weeks left for them to do that. "We'll give it a try." It was obvious that Mindy Carson did not know that the Lucky Dollar was probably going to have to be sold in order to raise the money with which to pay her.

"Please sit down," Mindy suggested, "and let me get you something cool to drink. I have iced tea or lemonade."

"Please don't go to any trouble," Lindsey said.

"It will be my pleasure. I don't get many guests to fawn over."

"Lemonade, then."

"Iced tea," J.L. requested, and Lindsey suppressed a sigh. They couldn't even agree on what to drink. Were they always going to be on opposite sides?

In looking around the humble lodgings of Mindy Carson, it was easy to see why this charming young woman needed the money she had discovered was owed her mother's estate, and Lindsey began to understand why J.L. had been so unrelenting in his demand for the thirty thousand dollars.

Mindy soon returned with frosted glasses of tea and lemonade for them and herself, and a plate of homemade oatmeal raisin cookies, which she graciously offered her guests.

"Tell Lindsey how you happen to be in a wheelchair," J.L. suggested, and Mindy explained, in a straightforward manner devoid of self-pity.

"I'm a paraplegic because of a motorcycle accident that happened three years ago. My bike slid out from under me and I fell over a cliff. Crashed about forty feet down." She gave a little laugh. "The bike was totaled and I didn't do much better."

Lindsey admired the young woman's candor.

"I've always been a bit of a daredevil," Mindy went on. "Try anything once, that's me. Was me. Like most people who ride motorcycles, I was convinced that nothing would ever happen to me. I was an excellent rider. I'd had my own dirt bike since I was ten years old, and the bike I was riding the day of the accident felt like an extension of my own body."

Lindsey shuddered, wondering how the trauma had changed Mindy's life, and J.L. supplied part of the answer. "Mindy was going to San Diego State at the time, majoring in art and history but, because of months of recuperation in the hospital and several required operations, she had to drop out."

"What do you do now?" Lindsey asked.

"I stuff envelopes for a company in San Francisco. It doesn't pay much, but at least I can afford to feed myself. My mother left me this house, and when I get the money from the Lucky Dollar—" She stopped. "I'm sorry, Lindsey. I'm sure that's a lot of money for you to part with, but it will be a godsend to me."

"Mindy needs it for more surgery and medical equipment to help her get around."

"I want to be a teacher someday, but I need a van that's converted for wheelchair use so I can drive myself and not have to depend on others."

"Do you have family nearby?" Lindsey asked, hoping she did.

Mindy looked down at her hands, but said nothing.

J.L. spoke up. "Mindy was married to a man who didn't understand the vows that said, 'For better or for worse, in sickness and in health.' After the accident, he divorced Mindy as soon as he could."

Mindy looked up into Lindsey's eyes. "It was hard for him to be married to a woman confined to a wheelchair. He's very active in sports...and other things."

Lindsey wanted to put her arms around the young woman. Even though they had just met, she already liked and respected

Mindy Carson. She was real, a fighter who wanted to support herself and didn't ask for pity from others.

"Is there a chance you'll walk again?" Lindsey had to ask.

Mindy's face brightened. "Yes, eventually, but it will take a lot of money, and time."

"And patience," J.L. added. He turned to Lindsey. "So you can see why Mindy needs all the money at once, not small amounts over a period of time. That money will help her recovery."

"Yes, I do understand, now," Lindsey admitted, and her eyes were soft when she looked at J.L.

She leaned over from her place on a lumpy, upholstered couch and squeezed Mindy's hands. "Your mother helped my father at a time when he desperately needed it. I'm happy to be able to repay the debt." And, strangely enough, she meant it. Mindy Carson deserved another chance.

❧

Driving home after their visit, neither J.L. nor Lindsey spoke for a while but then Lindsey broke the silence. "Mindy has really suffered these past few years, but look at her positive attitude. I like her determination to take care of herself. I'm sorry I was so resentful of her."

"Don't be hard on yourself." J.L. reached over and patted her hand where it lay on the seat. "You were fighting for your life, too."

"Well," Lindsey gave a wan smile, "you won't have to fight me anymore, Mr. Brett. You can start procedures to sell the mine as soon as you want. Mindy needs help now." She paused, and her eyes suddenly flashed. "I will, of course, still try to find the money on my own."

J.L. pulled her hand up to his lips and kissed her fingertips, slowly. "I hope you do. Believe that, Lindsey. And I respect you for honoring your father's debt."

Lindsey liked the feeling of self-respect that flooded through her, as well as the distinct pleasure of having J.L.'s admiration, but she still wasn't sure how it all would end. What if no buyer were found for the Lucky Dollar? She asked J.L. the question.

In answer, he put a cassette tape in to play. "This is one of my favorite songs. Listen to the words, Lindsey. They'll give you the answers you seek."

Lindsey listened as a rich baritone sang, "Great is Thy faithfulness! Great is Thy faithfulness! Morning by morning new mercies I see. All I have needed Thy hand hath provided. Great is Thy faithfulness, Lord, unto me! Pardon for sin and a peace that endureth. Thy own dear presence to cheer and to guide. Strength for today and bright hope for tomorrow— blessings all mine, with ten thousand beside!"*

Her eyes filled with tears. New as she was at being a Christian, she did believe that God would give her strength and hope. She had to trust in His faithfulness to guide her. After all, she was His child. He loved her.

When they arrived at her house, there was a package resting against the front door. It was small and wrapped exquisitely in gold foil and black-and-gold netting and silk ribbon.

"I wonder what this is?" Lindsey questioned, turning the package over and over in her hands while J.L. unlocked the front door with the key she had given him.

In the darkness that had come with the night, she could not see the set of his jaw harden or note the jealousy that narrowed his eyes. She did not know what was in the package, but J.L. suspected.

twenty-one

"Let me check the house and then I'll go," J.L. said to Lindsey, holding the door open for her.

"Out here we don't worry about people breaking in," she told him.

"The advantage of living in a small town. Still, you can never be too careful."

"You're right. Thank you."

J.L. walked quickly through each of her rooms to be sure there was no unwanted visitor, and to give Lindsey a chance to open the mysterious package.

"Oh, how sweet," he heard her murmur. He finished his inspection and joined her in the living room. She held up an exquisite half-ounce, tear-shaped bottle of perfume with a crystal dove on the top for him to see. "It's from Lance. *L'Air du Temps.*" She said the name with awe and tipped it over so the stopper would absorb some of the delicate floral and spice scent that she then dabbed behind her ears. "Mmm, it smells heavenly."

It ought to, J.L. thought, knowing the deeply romantic French scent, in its hand-blown Lalique crystal bottle, cost around $110.00 a quarter-ounce. He often bought this very perfume for his mother. Old Lance was lavishing quite a gift on the woman he hoped to marry. *Must have figured it would impress Lindsey, and it is.* J.L. wished it weren't.

He leaned over, close to her face, her shining hair touching his forehead. "You wear it well," he whispered, feeling a rush of emotion at her nearness and the tempting scent of her, but he stood back without taking advantage of the situation.

144

As he watched Lindsey's enchantment with her gift, turning the bottle around and around so that it caught the dazzling light from the table lamp, frustration knotted his stomach at the thought of Lance romancing Lindsey while he, J.L., lost out because of some antiquated ideal of ethics.

He doubted Lance Robards truly understood the woman he was pursuing. Lindsey was not ordinary. She was unique, exquisite, compassionate, charming, and courageous. She was also vulnerable at the moment, and J.L. prayed she would not be tempted to find the money to pay Mindy by marrying the shallow, self-interested restaurateur.

Wait for me, Lindsey, he told her with his eyes and with his heart. *Wait for me, and I'll marry you myself.*

&

"Lindsey, I need to talk with you," Santiago said, lumbering into the mine office two weeks after Lindsey's fateful meeting with Mindy Carson. His shirt was wet with perspiration from working on the sixth level of the mine where Lindsey had found some water seepage the day before and had sent him to check it out.

"I can't talk right now, Santiago, I've learned about a new bank in Escondido where I might get a loan for the Lucky Dollar." Her eyes were bright with excitement. "But look at all they want to know: business loan application, three years' tax returns, three years' balance sheets from the mine, list of outstanding debts, assets, liabilities." She picked up one paper after another on her desk and waved them at him. "I'm surprised they don't require a day-by-day account of my life from the moment I was born."

Santiago chuckled.

"Can we talk when I get back?" she asked, slinging a black patent-leather purse over the shoulder of her green linen business suit and taking up several file folders into her arms. "I'm on my way to the bank now and after that to see Mindy Carson in San Diego." She had told him about Mindy. "What's the situation on the water?"

"We found the problem," Santiago answered, following her brisk walk out the door. "The men are working on it now. But I really need to talk to you."

They reached the parking lot and Lindsey got into her red two-door Cherokee. "I'm sorry, Santiago, but I must fly." She gave him an apologetic smile. "Later?"

He shrugged. "Sure, it can wait, I guess. It's probably not a good idea anyway."

Lindsey turned on the ignition, shifted into gear, and the tires of the Jeep kicked up some gravel as she drove away.

Santiago watched her go. Then he stuffed his hands in the pockets of his jeans, and shuffled slowly back to the mine.

⋆

It was long after dark when Lindsey got home and remembered she had promised to talk to Santiago. "Oh well, it's too late to call him now. I'll see him tomorrow," and she went to bed but couldn't sleep because she kept comparing J.L. with Lance.

She had seen her would-be fiancè several times since he had come to the mine, and she had thanked him profusely for the perfume. More and more, however, he had succeeded in turning her off. His continual put-down of Christians and his unwillingness to understand what the mine meant to her, made her wonder why she even spent time with him.

The main goal of his life was the acquisition of things and position and reputation. Though he was, basically, a nice man, there was not enough depth to him to interest her.

J.L., on the other hand, was a whole different story. While he wasn't against the wealthy life he had inherited and was living, the joy in his life came from doing for others. It gave him power and respect, to be sure, but that's not why he did what he did. His motive was simple: if people needed help, he wanted to be there.

In her darkened bedroom, Lindsey pulled the covers up to

her chin and gazed through the tall window at the moon out-side. It splashed a benevolent path of silvery light across her bed and focused her thoughts on J.L. She had told him, "You won't have to fight me anymore...sell the mine as soon as you want. Mindy needs help now. I will, of course, still try to find the money on my own." She murmured out loud, "I sure hope this bank in Escondido comes through for me."

Snuggling deeper into the covers and closing her eyes, she recounted how much she admired J.L.—his strength, his hu-mor, his rugged manliness that thrilled her heart. Did he re-ally want to start a relationship with her when their legal situ-ation was settled? She hoped so. Oh, how she hoped so.

ഛ

The next morning Lindsey was glad to see Santiago already in the mine office when she arrived. He had made coffee and she drank deeply from her first cup and said, "Okay, Santiago, what did you want to talk with me about?"

The big man eased himself down into the chair in front of her desk and took a deep breath. "You look nice, boss," he said.

"Thanks." She felt comfortable in a cool and feminine cu-cumber-colored jumpsuit of rayon and polyester, a paisley scarf around her neck. "I may be going back to the bank in Escondido this afternoon. Surprisingly, they said it might take only twenty-four hours to make up their minds on my loan request. The other banks took a week or two."

Santiago bent forward, leaning massive, hairy arms on the old wooden desk. Taking a deep breath, he said, "You don't have to wait for that bank, boss. I have the thirty thousand dollars."

"Mmm?" she answered distractedly, for she was pulling pa-pers out of the file drawer in her desk.

"I have thirty thousand dollars and you can have it to pay back the loan, and the mine won't have to be sold."

Lindsey's hands froze in midair, holding a manila folder

with a red label on one corner. Looking up and into Santiago's eyes, she could tell he was nervous, and also thought she had heard him wrong. "What did you say?" she questioned.

"I can lend you the thirty thousand."

"Lend me…?"

"Maria and I have been saving a thousand dollars a year ever since I started working at this mine."

"That's admirable, Santiago."

"I don't want the mine to be sold. I don't want to look for another job."

"New owners might keep you on."

"Might and might not. I don't want to take any chances and I don't want to work for anyone but you. Better yet, you can have our thirty thousand dollars in exchange for a partnership in the mine."

Lindsey's mouth slowly opened wider and wider and she offered no dissent.

"I'm getting up in age, Lindsey, and I want to know there will be money for Maria and me when it's time to retire. Right now the mine isn't producing a whole lot more than what keeps all of us living a fairly decent life, but there's always that chance that we'll find the Mother Lode, or at least another big strike.

"You and your father have been good to me and Maria through the years. You and the Lucky Dollar are like family to us. So take the money. Keep the mine and give me a shot at a good future."

Lindsey exploded out of her chair and charged around the desk, flinging herself into his arms. "Oh, Santiago, you're a lifesaver. What a brilliant plan—for the mine as well as yourself. Yes, yes, yes. Let's do it. Let's keep the Lucky Dollar… together."

An unbelieving grin began on the heavy lips of the old foreman, and expanded into a broad, incredulous smile, then into a deep belly laugh.

"Really, boss? You like the idea?"

"Oh, Santiago, it's perfect. I'd be thrilled to know that after more than thirty years of faithful service to the Lucky Dollar it would give you back a safe and comfortable retirement. How wise you and Maria were to save your money a little each year."

She backed away now, a little embarrassed at how she had overwhelmed him, but still wanting him to know how thrilled she was with his suggestion. "You *are* the Lucky Dollar, Santiago," she told him. "You belong to each other." Her eyes glistened with tears. "Are you absolutely sure you want to do this? There is always the chance that the mine will fizzle out today, tomorrow, next year."

He was still smiling. "I know that, and Maria knows that, but we want to stay where we are, in that house where we raised our children, and I want to keep working the mine. I figure I still have a good ten years left in me and I'll feel like a million dollars walking through the tunnels, knowing a percentage of them belong to me."

He got serious then. "I've never owned anything much in my life, Lindsey, except that beat-up old truck I drive. I don't even own that house that you let me live in. It would make me proud to have a part of the mine to show for a life's work, and to leave to my children. I want them, and Maria, to be proud of me."

Lindsey began to cry. "Santiago, you are so precious. I know for a fact how proud your children, and Maria, too, are of you already. You're a good man, a faithful, hard-working man."

Santiago stepped back and stuck out his hand. "So, is it a deal?"

Lindsey did not hesitate for a moment. She pushed her hand into his and said, "Yes, sir. We'll get John Gregory to draw up papers after we figure out what a fair percentage would be for you to own in exchange for your money."

"It doesn't have to be much—"

"It has to be fair," Lindsey insisted, pointing a finger at him.

"Okay, boss."

"Partner," Lindsey corrected firmly, then wiped her eyes and stared at her foreman. "Santiago, you have made me a very happy woman."

So, later that morning Santiago appeared back in the mine office with a cashier's check for thirty thousand dollars. "But Santiago, we haven't signed any papers yet," Lindsey said.

"We shook hands. That's enough."

"We're still going to write this up legally, though," Lindsey told him.

"I know, but I wanted you to have this as soon as possible," he countered. "Now your heart can be at ease."

Lindsey gave him an enthusiastic kiss on the cheek. "How does it feel to be a lifesaver?" she asked him, and Santiago just grinned from ear to ear and stuck out his barrel chest even further than normal.

ꝫ

Lindsey drove to San Diego, singing. On her way to J.L.'s office, she smiled at every person she passed, even Heather, who looked at her warily, wondering if anything would be broken today because of her visit. It pleased Heather to announce, "I'm sorry, but Mr. Brett is not here. He's in Los Angeles on a case."

"When will he be back?" Lindsey asked, disappointed. She had been looking forward to seeing the expression on J.L.'s face when she handed him the check for thirty thousand dollars.

"Day after tomorrow."

"I see."

Reluctantly, Lindsey took an envelope from her purse. "Please give him this, then, and tell him who it's from." She added, "Have him call me, please. Immediately."

Heather accepted the envelope with a question in her eyes. Whatever could be inside? She hoped it wasn't a flat little bomb that would explode in J.L.'s face when he opened it.

twenty-two

Lindsey left J.L.'s office in buoyant but reflective spirits. What a totally unexpected way the mine situation had been resolved. Everyone was a winner: she was, the mine, its employees, Santiago, Mindy…but what about her relationship with J.L.?

He had told her on the day of Santiago's birthday party that, until the case was settled, it was not ethical for him to pursue her. He had also said, "I'm attracted to you…a lot…I keep wanting to be with you."

As to her part in all this, she remembered telling him that once the Lucky Dollar was sold, she wasn't sure she would want to have anything to do with him. Now that things would soon be settled, she could tell him the truth that she was in love with him…sensibly, rationally, deliriously, wildly in love with him.

How could she not love this man of high principle and singular determination who, at a single touch, could set her mind, heart, and body into a turmoil? One look from those dark, penetrating eyes, and she melted. One word with that voice that was made for Shakespeare, and she soared to heaven.

He cared about the same things she did—people and God. His quiet Christian life showed her a way that was new and uncertain to her, but she knew she could trust him. Trust his judgment. Even if she had lost the mine, she would still have loved him.

Slamming the door of the Jeep after she got in, Lindsey knew her life would be unsettled until she could talk to J.L. face to face and explain where she had gotten the thirty thousand dollars to save the mine. *Won't he be surprised?* she giggled in anticipation of their next meeting.

In the meantime, since he was out of town, she decided she needed a vacation and, when she got home, she called a quiet bed-and-breakfast inn she had stayed at before on Santa Catalina Island, twenty-six miles off the southern California coast, and made a reservation for a few days. It was the perfect place to relax until J.L. returned. She wanted to be her best for him, when they started their relationship.

≥∞

J.L. charged up the path to the mine office, flung open the door, nearly taking it off its hinges, again, and startled Santiago who was sitting at Lindsey's desk, going over the accounts. Lindsey had wanted him to familiarize himself with the paperwork involved in running the mine.

"Where is she?" J.L. demanded to know.

Santiago rose to his feet and folded his arms across his wide chest. "Miss Lindsey isn't here," he answered firmly, not liking the wild look in the lawyer's eyes.

J.L. placed both hands on the desk and leaned forward on them. "Don't protect her, Santiago. I have to see her. Did you know she brought a check for thirty thousand dollars to my office?"

Santiago shook his head yes.

"So I have to talk with her about it. Where is she?"

"Miss Lindsey's gone."

"Gone? Where?"

"On vacation."

"What?" The word exploded from J.L.'s mouth and he slammed one hand down hard on the desk. A small clock tumbled off one corner and clattered on the floor.

Santiago frowned. "Is there anything else I can help you with, Mr. Brett?"

J.L. took a deep breath and let it out all at once. "She's with *him*, isn't she? I hadn't expected he'd move so fast. The snake.

He gave her the money to save her mine and thinks she'll marry him in gratitude. But she won't. She can't. She doesn't love him, I know that. I *know* that!"

He slammed his other hand down on the desk, and a vase with dried flowers in it flew off one side and shattered into a dozen pieces when it hit the floor.

Santiago did not move, nor correct J.L.'s erroneous conception as to where the money had come from; that was Lindsey's prerogative.

"Why didn't I tell her a long time ago that I love her?" he flung the words at Santiago, but he wasn't really talking to him; he was talking to himself. "I started falling in love with her the very first day I met her, when she nearly killed me, shooting at that mountain lion. I'd never seen so spunky a woman. I'd never been so intrigued by a personality. I was attracted to her uniqueness, her spirit, her fire, her vulnerability, her precious Christian faith."

His pacing quickened, and with his long and powerful legs it took only a few strides to go from wall to wall in the small office.

"I told myself I couldn't pursue her. That it wasn't ethical as long as I was representing an opposing client. But I kept wanting to be with her." He whirled to face Santiago. "You can understand that, can't you? I mean, what man wouldn't fall in love with Lindsey Faraday after five minutes with her."

Santiago nodded in agreement and began to grin.

"Now I've probably lost her," J.L. declared and, with the flat of a hand, he smacked the nearest wall. A picture fell off and the glass broke on the floor.

Santiago finally came from behind the desk and grabbed J.L. by the shoulders. "Before you destroy this office, I'm going to tell you where Lindsey is. She went to Catalina. To a bed-and-breakfast inn on Metropole Avenue."

A roar like that of a wounded beast shook the little office to its foundation. "She's with him, isn't she? I know she is. Well, while I have a breath in my body, he's not going to seduce the woman I love!"

J.L. whirled around and crashed into an old wooden chair, which splintered and fell to the floor, destroyed. A furious groan accompanied his race to the door, which he tore open but not off its hinges, and Santiago chuckled as he watched the lawyer storm down the path to save his lady love from a fate worse than death, which didn't even exist.

⤷

J.L. was an irate and determined man with a mission: find Lindsey and save her from Lance Robards. They didn't belong together. They saw life from opposite ends of the telescope. Robards was materialistic; Lindsey was idealistic.

He condemned Robards for taking advantage of Lindsey's predicament and buying himself a wife who would never love him and whom he could never satisfy.

J.L. ached for Lindsey who had been so desperate to keep her mine and the jobs of a few people who were dear to her that she had sold herself and her future for money.

All these thoughts churned relentlessly through J.L.'s mind as he drove frantically from the mine back to his home in La Jolla, threw a few things into an overnight bag, caught a two o'clock flight out of San Diego, endured the thirty-minute flight, chafed at the twenty minutes or so it took the bus to go from the Airport-in-the-Sky into Avalon, the tiny principal town of 1500 on the island, and from there to walk the short distance to Metropole Avenue where he found the Sunset Inn.

It was a blazing hot day, under a merciless sun (the sun shone 267 days a year on Catalina), and his shirt had dampened considerably during his travels as he pushed himself to reach the inn and confront Robards. He wasn't tired, though. Relentless energy had driven him across the ocean to rescue the woman he loved.

"I'm looking for Lindsey Faraday," he told the pretty blond woman who answered the door at the inn.

"Come in," she invited. "She's not here right now, but should be back shortly. She's parasailing."

J.L. followed her into a cheerful sun-splashed living room with windows on three walls through which could be seen a thick green lawn dotted with white, wrought-iron benches, the riotous red and purple flowers of a bougainvillea vine, and a spectacular view of the Pacific Ocean and boats bobbing in Avalon Bay.

The young woman smiled. "Are you looking for a room or only for Lindsey?"

"I'd better have a room," he told her.

"For how many nights?"

J.L. didn't hesitate. "One, to start with. I may go home tomorrow."

"That's too bad."

"Or I might stay longer." *Depending on whether or not I'm wanted for murdering Lance Robards,* he considered. He thought of asking for Robards, but assumed he was with Lindsey, and even if he weren't, J.L. wanted to talk with Lindsey first.

Taking a key from the desk drawer, the young woman started up some stairs and J.L. followed, toting his overnight bag. "We'll put you in the Sunflower Room," she said. "It has one of the finest views of the ocean and a king-size bed."

She led him into a dazzling room decorated in warm yellow and white, with white wicker chairs and white-and-yellow-striped curtains that did not diminish the view from the large window.

"Feel free to cool off in our pool and have some lemonade and freshly baked cookies until Lindsey gets back," his hostess suggested.

"Sounds great."

J.L. was hot and sweaty and had been knotted up for hours. He needed to relax before he met Lindsey. He didn't want to scare her, or do anything he would regret to Lance Robards.

He swam laps for twenty minutes, but even the warm water of the pool did not ease the tension he felt all over his body. He didn't enjoy the soft lounge chair or the lemonade or the sugar cookies.

He paced, around the pool, back and forth, not even noticing the pleasant breeze that drifted over the hillside and played with the ends of his hair. He tried to read a magazine, but couldn't concentrate, so he sat and stared at the ocean in the distance and waited for the happy couple.

Twenty minutes later, his vigil was rewarded. Looking through his dark sunglasses, he saw Lindsey strolling toward the diving board. Over her bathing suit she was wearing a wrap that, when she reached the board, she unfastened and tossed onto a nearby chair. Robards was not with her.

J.L. admired her slim figure and golden angel hair that hung straight, below her shoulders. She was one beautiful woman, tanned and firm and appealing in a cranberry red suit that had only one strap over her left shoulder. He swallowed hard and rose from the chair.

The water made little sound when Lindsey cleanly dove into it, swam half the length of the pool before surfacing, then did a breast stroke to the end where she looked up and saw a pair of muscular legs leading up to narrow hips and a black bathing suit on a man whose chest was far from narrow and whose face she recognized with shock.

J.L.

He leaned over and extended a hand, and Lindsey eagerly took it. The dream of their being together, finally, flowered deep within her as his strong hand enfolded hers. The relationship they had denied each other through the last torturous months was about to begin, possible now because J.L. had her check for thirty thousand dollars. He had probably already delivered it to Mindy.

As he effortlessly hoisted her up, Lindsey smiled exuberantly, but when her wet feet found the deck, and she saw the scowl on his face, she lost her concentration and slipped. One of J.L.'s arms flew around her waist and brought her against the dry, hot length of him. Their skin touching, Lindsey looked into his eyes and he into hers and she wondered why he wasn't kissing her.

"Lindsey. We have to talk."

twenty-three

J.L. released Lindsey and gestured toward a white wrought iron table. Lindsey, unsure of why his attitude was chilly toward her, nodded her approval, and they went over to the table and sat down.

In a flash, J.L. recalled how he had felt just that morning when he had gone into his office and Heather had handed him Lindsey's check for thirty thousand dollars. He had been dumbfounded.

"Did she leave me a note with this?" he had asked his secretary.

"No."

"A verbal message?"

"Nothing."

J.L. had thought for a moment, scratching his chin. *Where did she get the money?* he had asked himself over and over until a light had dawned. There was no other explanation. Lindsey must not have been able to get financing to save the mine, so she had taken the only course open to her—she was going to marry Lance Robards and get the money from him. Mostly for the sake of her employees, whom she loved and hovered over like a mother hen, she was sacrificing her future in order to secure theirs.

Of course, he didn't know this for sure. She might have found another source, but a gut feeling he couldn't deny believed only that.

So, he had gone after her, like the cavalry to the rescue. He was going to save her from ruining her life, show her what a cad Lance Robards was for taking advantage of her desperate need, be her hero and carry her off and tell her he loved her and claim her for himself. He was even going to offer to pay the thirty thousand dollars to save the mine. She would then be free to marry him. Him, not Robards.

But all the words he had rehearsed, all the emotions he had yearned to express, suddenly fled him as he faced her, here on this island paradise of flowers and ocean and playful breezes, her eyes crystal blue and questioning. His stomach did flip-flops as he suddenly remembered something she had told him just a few weeks before. She had said, "How can you think I would marry a man I don't love just to get my hands on his money?" But she had. The check proved it.

He was angry with her...with her...her.

Until this moment, all his outrage had been against Robards, as though the man had forced Lindsey to accept him against her will. Now, as J.L. sat and looked at Lindsey, aching to take her in his arms, longing to taste her lips, yearning to tell her of his feelings for her, he realized she must have willingly agreed to the plan. She was too strong minded, too independent, too intelligent to be persuaded to do something she did not want to do.

"If this debt of my father's is legitimate," she had told him once, "then it shall be paid, no matter what it takes to do so." That she would go into marriage for such a wrong reason, bothered J.L. For her to put more priority on a possession, the mine, than on the sanctity of a lifetime relationship, made J.L. think he might have made a mistake in thinking Lindsey was a sincere Christian.

Still, one small voice urged him to reconsider. Maybe she did get the money from a bank. She deserved the benefit of the doubt, didn't she?

So, instead of telling her he loved her, and wanted her, he gave her a chance and said simply, "I have the check."

"Good," Lindsey responded with a smile.

"He gave it to you, didn't he?" J.L. asked, "he" meaning Robards.

"Yes, he did. Wasn't it wonderful of him?" "Him" meaning Santiago.

"Wouldn't a bank lend you the money?"

"I tried as many as would even give me an application, J.L. When I called the last one, in Escondido, to let them know I didn't need the loan anymore, I found out that it, too, was going to turn me down."

J.L. was really put off by her cheerful attitude. How could she be happy over a forthcoming marriage of convenience? Unless…unless…she really cared for Robards.

"Is this really what you want?" he asked, leaning forward, giving her one more chance to break down and sob out her unfortunate plight and beg him to rescue her.

Instead, she gave him a look of amazement. "Of course it is. How could you doubt it? You know what the mine means to me. This offer was a godsend."

J.L. felt sick to his stomach. Instead of holding her in his arms and telling her he loved her and wanted her desperately and would she please mark off a few hours on her calendar one day next month so that they could get married, he had lost her. He had waited too long, and lost her.

"Did you give the money to Mindy?" Lindsey asked.

"Uh, no, not yet. I just got it this morning; I've been out of town."

"Yes, I know. Mindy's a wonderful person, isn't she? So genuine and positive. I'm glad it's worked out for her. And the Lucky Dollar."

She leaned over the table toward him, her wet hair hanging within a few inches of J.L.'s hand, presenting a temptation he found hard to resist. "Aren't you thrilled with how all of this has turned out?" she asked.

J.L. sprang to his feet, pushing the chair back with his legs.

"Thrilled is not the word I'd use," he growled. "More like appalled."

Lindsey stared up at him through the bright sunshine. "Appalled? What does that mean, J.L.?"

He wanted to grab her and shake her until her teeth rattled. Her unflappable calm in the face of the degrading alliance she had made galled him.

"You want to know what's the matter?" he roared. "Well, lady, for starters, I can't believe you stooped so low to get your hands on that money—"

Lindsey rose to her feet. "It was graciously offered to me—"

"Graciously? You mean you didn't grovel for it?."

"Certainly not. The offer was a sensible one that I'm thrilled with, if you must know."

"A sensible business deal, in other words."

"Yes, and no one deserves it more than him. He's been so good to me."

J.L.'s eyes almost fell out of his head. "How good?"

"Why, with his time and devotion—"

"Garbage!"

Lindsey plastered her hands on her hips. "I cannot believe your reaction to this, J.L. Why aren't you delighted the money has been paid? That means you've won. What difference does it make where the funds came from?"

J.L. rolled his eyes as though he had been struck by a frying pan. "I thought you were a woman of principle, Lindsey, a woman who would not compromise when it came to her integrity."

Lindsey gasped. "Compromise? You call it compromise to accept the offer of help from a man I think the world of?"

"So you have strong feelings for him?"

"I adore him."

J.L. gaped at her, then stumbled over to the pool and stared down into it.

Lindsey followed him, her temper rising. "This man is one in a million. I couldn't ask for anyone more perfect for a partner."

J.L. whirled around and faced her. "Then you're a fool!" He threw the words at her before he had a chance to think.

Lindsey's eyes flashed. "Santiago has given most of his adult life to that mine and he deserves a solid retirement. I just hope his partnership in the mine will do that. If you think I'm a fool for giving him that, then you're a heartless man."

She whirled and started to walk away, but J.L. grabbed her wrist and turned her back to him. "Santiago? Why are we talking about him?"

"We've been talking about him all along, J.L."

"Santiago?" J.L. hit the side of his forehead with the heel of his hand. "Santiago gave you the money?"

"I've been telling you that for ten minutes."

"I thought you got it from Lance Robards. That you agreed to marry him—"

"What?" The word exploded out of Lindsey's mouth and she took two steps backward. "You believe I agreed to marry Lance Robards just to get the money to save the mine?"

"Yes."

"You think I have so little regard for myself? No more dignity than a hopeless beggar? No more respect for the sacrament of marriage? Oooooooo."

"Now, don't get upset, Lindsey. I misunderstood, that's all."

"Misunderstood? If you knew me at all, you could never have *misunderstood.*"

J.L. reached out and placed both hands on her waist. "I have something to tell you, Lindsey, now that I know you're not really going to marry Lance Robards." He bent to kiss her, but Lindsey slammed both her hands on his hard-breathing chest and gave him a shove—backward, into the shimmering water.

He came up sputtering. "Hey, what was that for?"

"It was my way of saying goodbye, J.L. Brett. I hope I never set eyes on you again. Never hear your disgusting voice. If I could, I'd move off the planet to keep from being within a million miles of you!"

Lindsey spun on her heels and stormed off toward the inn. Ignoring calls from J.L. to come back, she dashed up the stairs that led to her room, threw her belongings into her suitcase, stopped at the hostess's room just long enough to tell her she was leaving, ran the several blocks into Avalon and to the dock, and took the last boat leaving for the mainland.

Seventy minutes later, with the millions of lights of Long Beach magnificently dancing in welcome to the returning vacationers, Lindsey left the boat, got her car from the parking lot, and drove all the way to Majestic, without shedding one tear. She was too furious to cry.

But she did pray. *Oh, Lord, great is Your faithfulness. I thank You for helping me to keep the mine. I also thank You for letting me see just what kind of man J.L. Brett is and keeping me from making a mistake over him. I've always been content with the Lucky Dollar as the love of my life, and that's the way it will be from now on.*

Then she cried.

twenty-four

"You actually accused Lindsey of agreeing to marry Lance Robards, just to pay off the debt of the mine?" Santiago asked J.L., then listened in disbelief to J.L.'s confession. They were standing in the office of the Lucky Dollar the day after the fateful confrontation on Catalina.

"Pretty stupid, eh?"

"It just proves you don't know her very well."

"But I want to, Santiago. I love her, and want to marry her."

Santiago smiled. "Then go after her. Apologize as you've never apologized before. She'll forgive you."

"How do you know?"

"I just know. For some reason only understood by God and women, they love us men in spite of ourselves."

"I'm not sure she loves me, or will even speak to me."

"Then you speak to her. Don't let her get away or you'll be sorry the rest of your life."

"Good idea. Do you know where she is?"

"Try the mine. She's been sulking in there all day."

"Thanks, Santiago." J.L. stuck out his hand and vigorously shook the foreman's. "I'm glad you're investing in the mine. I think it will do well for you."

"Me, too. Now, if you'll excuse me, I've got things to do. Partners are busy people."

With a big grin, J.L. slapped Santiago on the back and ran out the door and down the rocky hillside toward the mine, but skidded to a stop when he saw a tawny brown mountain lion, big and stealthy, entering the mine, crouched and cautious, expecting to find something to satisfy his hunger.

"Lindsey," J.L. gasped under his breath.

164

Whirling around, he sped back to the mine office, grabbed the rifle from the corner behind the desk where Lindsey kept it, checked to see that it was loaded, and, as he raced out, yelled, "Mountain lion!" to Santiago.

When he entered the mine it was dark and silent and he saw no sign of the cat, nor heard it, either.

Where was Lindsey? There were dozens of tunnels she could be in, and he barely knew his way through the main one. What if she were on another level and he couldn't get to her in time? The thought of that huge cat mauling her, drawing blood, made every hair on J.L.'s body stand on end.

He crouched, and silently advanced, stopping every few feet to listen and let his eyes adjust to the darkness.

He remembered where Lindsey kept a flashlight not far from the entrance, found it, and turned it on. He had no idea where light switches were, or even if there were some all along the way. Even if the light from the flashlight distracted the big cat, that was okay. Better it attack him than Lindsey. He was bigger than she and he had the gun. She was helpless and unaware that she was being stalked.

Then he heard it—the soft growl. It didn't sound far off, so he inched his way forward as quietly as he could, not knowing if he could surprise the big cat, but certain that that might be the only chance Lindsey would have, and he had to give it to her.

J.L. stepped cautiously, wishing he were wearing tennis shoes. Stalking a hungry cougar, while wearing a business suit and slick-soled shoes, was not an everyday occurrence for him. Fortunately, he had always had good balance and, as he took step after careful step, powerful muscles in his thighs and calves kept him from sliding as the terrain descended, further and further into the darkness.

He followed the sounds from the cat, down a ramp, around a corner. A sudden flap of wings—bats—startled him and he dropped the flashlight. It went out and cold, gut-wrenching terror gripped his insides. Frantically groping for the light, he could not even see his own hand in front of his face. He was holding his breath and he had never felt so alone.

Then his fingers connected with metal and he grabbed the flashlight and turned it on just as he heard a snarling sound followed by a heart-stopping roar then a piercing female scream.

"Lindsey!" he yelled at the top of his voice. "I'm coming!"

He tripped and fell, but still had the flashlight in his hand and, though his skin was torn from his scraping himself on the dirt floor of the mine, he got up, feeling no pain in his body but sheer panic in his heart.

He rounded a corner and there they were, in a jump hole where, "in the old days," Lindsey had explained once, "when a miner heard the roar of an approaching mine car, he had to get out of the way, so 'jump holes' were dug out from place to place in the walls for safety's sake."

Lindsey was in such a jump hole now, illuminated by a single light bulb. She was squatting on a small plank desk whose top was covered with various field tests and measurement equipment, papers and pencils, and a telephone.

In her hand was a long stick that she was using to fend off the cat who was pawing at it from the ground and growling fiercely, baring its teeth.

Instantly, with smooth reflexive motion, J.L. raised and aimed the rifle just as the cat became aware he was there. The big beast forgot Lindsey and leaped for J.L. instead, who pulled the trigger while the animal was in midair.

The awful thud of one bullet and then another, impacting with thick flesh, was amplified a hundred times in the narrow confines of the tunnel. The cat crashed to the floor and an eerie silence followed.

Then Lindsey sobbed and leaped from the table and threw herself into J.L.'s arms. Still holding the rifle, he crushed her against him, burying his face in the lush thickness of her hair.

"Oh, J.L.," she cried, "you saved my life. I thought I was going to die, and all I could think of was that I loved you but had never told you, and how silly I had been to be angry with you over the money. You made an honest mistake and I blew it all out of proportion. I love you. Oh, I love you."

She was babbling and crying, and J.L. held her close, thanking God that she was alive.

They clutched each other frantically, and not even when they heard the pounding of running footsteps, did they separate.

Santiago and two other men tore around the last corner and stopped dead when they saw the big cat lying across the path and Lindsey firmly in J.L.'s arms as though they were attached to each other.

"Are you all right, Lindsey?" Santiago asked frantically.

"She's fine," J.L. answered for her, and Lindsey raised her tear-stained face enough to nod agreement to her foreman.

"This is the same cat that's been destroying cattle near here," one of the men said, leaning over the beast, examining it to be sure it was dead. "Here's the peculiar white marking over its right eye."

Santiago confirmed the identity.

Slowly, Lindsey extricated herself from J.L. and walked over to the lion. She fell to the floor, on her knees, and amazingly, for someone who had just been threatened with death by this very creature, ran her hand over his beautiful fur.

She addressed it: "I know why you killed those cattle. We humans kept encroaching on your territory, building homes and towns, and your food supply disappeared. What else could you do but survive any way you could?" She sobbed and whispered, "I'm sorry," and then looked up at J.L. and he came to her, helped her up, and Santiago and the men picked up the mountain lion and carried it away.

J.L. gently enfolded Lindsey into his arms and whispered brokenly, "If I'd lost you, Lindsey...."

She clung to him and their mutual tears blended on their cheeks.

&

Two nights later, Lindsey and J.L. were back in the mine, approaching the Third Level where the lion had attacked Lindsey.

"I want you to see the place again," J.L. told her, "and not be afraid of it."

Lindsey squeezed his hand and gazed adoringly up at him. "Like getting back on a horse after being thrown?"

"Yeah."

They found the jump hole, and stood looking at the desk and scattered instruments, silhouetted in the muted darkness. After a few minutes Lindsey said, "I'm okay," and J.L. put his arm around her and led her away, but not toward the surface.

"Where are we going?" she asked, and then stopped. "I hear music. Why is there music?"

"You'll see," J.L. promised.

They rounded a bend and Lindsey stopped abruptly and took in a breath.

"It's about time you got here," Santiago said with mock censure. "The Beef Wellington is drying out."

Lindsey gaped at what she saw—a table covered with a crisp, white cloth and adorned with lit candles in silver holders and placed around a lavish bowl of pink rosebuds, and covered dishes, like one gets in a hotel with room service, from which the most delicious odors were emanating. Romantic music from a tape recorder played in the background.

"Thanks for keeping an eye on things, Santiago," J.L. said, shaking the man's hand.

"Any time," he answered with a wink that Lindsey caught. "Any time."

With a flourish J.L. pulled out one of the two chairs and motioned for Lindsey to sit down. She did, in a state of shock.

"We should eat while everything's hot," J.L. instructed, taking the cloth napkin from beside her china plate, shaking it open, and laying it with great flair over her lap.

She laughed. "You're crazy, do you know that?"

"Crazy in love, with you," he murmured, leaning over to kiss her on the lips.

Lindsey giggled and looked up at Santiago. "Are you joining us, partner?"

Santiago grinned. "Can't, Lindsey. I've got things to do." He walked away.

"And so do you," J.L. told Lindsey as he lifted the covers off the four dishes and insisted she begin a dinner fit for a queen.

Lindsey ate the gourmet food hungrily, as did J.L., but they both knew the best was yet to come. Seldom looking elsewhere but into each other's eyes, they ate and listened to the soft, dreamy music drifting through the narrow tunnel while the flickering candles created intimate shadows that danced off the surrounding rocky, sedimentary walls.

"Enjoying yourself?" J.L. asked, rolling part of an artichoke heart into his mouth.

Lindsey nodded her head. "You're very imaginative."

"Thank you."

"And romantic."

Lindsey knew she was living a dream, with this extraordinary man she loved above anything else in this world, even the Lucky Dollar. She got up and went around the table to J.L., who rose to accept her into his arms. They held each other, then J.L. kissed her, and she kissed him back.

"Does this mean we're starting our relationship?" Lindsey asked.

J.L. laughed softly. "I think we started it the first day we met each other, only we didn't know it."

"Or admit it."

He held her face between his strong hands. "Lindsey, I love you more than life. You are everything I admire in a person. You're honest and hardworking, thoughtful of others, loyal—"

"You make me sound like Girl Scout of the Year."

He kissed the tip of her nose. "There's nothing wrong with being good. It shines around you and makes me want to protect you from anything bad."

"Are you saying I need a guardian?"

He gathered her into his arms again. "No. I'm asking if you'll take me as a husband, a husband who thinks you're the most beautiful, enticing, enchanting female he's ever encountered."

Lindsey leaned back and gave him a teasing grin. "Did you put those words on that infamous list of yours that describes me?"

J.L. laughed out loud. "Those and a hundred more like feisty, unpredictable, smart—"

"Maker of the world's best chili?"

He coughed. "That's debatable. Come here, you," and he kissed her long and with great feeling. "I'll be incomplete without you, Lindsey. Please say yes to my proposal."

Lindsey giggled. "What proposal?"

"To marry me." He kissed her.

Lindsey slipped her arms around his neck and looked into dark, smoldering eyes that made her heart dance. "I love you, J.L. Brett, for all the same reasons you gave for loving me." She sighed and caught his lower lip gently between her teeth. "Yes, I will marry you, as long as you don't mind my owning a gold mine."

"Of course not. In case I ever decide to stop working, you can support me comfortably."

Lindsey groaned, then slowly traced the planes and curves of his face with her fingers. "Tell me again that you love me, J.L.," she murmured, her eyes filled with love for him.

He gave her a crooked smile that brought out his dimples, which she adored. "I love you, Lindsey Faraday, today, tomorrow, and forever. I will always be faithful to you."

"As God is faithful."

"Yes," and he captured her lips again and again, with growing fervency, there in the dimly lit tunnel, and neither of them noticed, or cared, that the dinner got cold and the candles burned down.

But the music played on.

A Letter To Our Readers

Dear Reader:

In order that we might better contribute to your reading enjoyment, we would appreciate your taking a few minutes to respond to the following questions. When completed, please return to the following:

Rebecca Germany, Editor
Heartsong Presents
P.O. Box 719
Uhrichsville, Ohio 44683

1. Did you enjoy reading *Golden Dreams*?
   - ❏ Very much. I would like to see more books
     by this author!
   - ❏ Moderately
     I would have enjoyed it more if _____

     _____

2. Are you a member of **Heartsong Presents**? ❏ Yes ❏ No
   If no, where did you purchase this book? _____

   _____

3. What influenced your decision to purchase this
   book? (Check those that apply.)

❏ Cover	❏ Back cover copy
❏ Title	❏ Friends
❏ Publicity	❏ Other_____

4. How would you rate, on a scale from 1 (poor) to 5
   (superior), the cover design? _____

5. On a scale from 1 (poor) to 10 (superior), please rate the following elements.

    ___ Heroine   ___ Plot

    ___ Hero   ___ Inspirational theme

    ___ Setting   ___ Secondary characters

6. What settings would you like to see covered in **Heartsong Presents** books?_____

_____

_____

7. What are some inspirational themes you would like to see treated in future books?_____

_____

_____

8. Would you be interested in reading other **Heartsong Presents** titles?   ❏ Yes   ❏ No

9. Please check your age range:
    ❏ Under 18   ❏ 18-24   ❏ 25-34
    ❏ 35-45   ❏ 46-55   ❏ Over 55

10. How many hours per week do you read? _____

Name _____

Occupation _____

Address _____

City_____ State_____ Zip _____

Kathleen Yapp

___*A New Song*—Opera star Serena Lawrence may lose her voice, but will she lose something even more valuable? Will Serena and Steve, a dynamic small-town minister, be able to fight their fears together or will they be denied the rich promise of a lifetime of love? HP70 $2.95

___*A Match Made in Heaven*—C. G. Grady doesn't want to meet the man her mother is sure will make the perfect husband. Drake Forrest refuses to meet the woman his matchmaking mother says will make the perfect wife. But mothers can't arrange a meeting like this. HP97 $2.95

___*Golden Dreams*—A mysterious woman lays a claim against Lindsey Faraday's Lucky Dollar Gold Mine. Representing the woman legally is the ruggedly handsome J. L. Brett, who all too quickly finds himself torn between responsibility and love. HP 162 $2.95

Heart♥ng

·········· Presents ··········

Great Inspirational Romance at a Great Price!

Heartsong Presents books are inspirational romances in contemporary and historical settings, designed to give you an enjoyable, spirit-lifting reading experience. You can choose from 164 wonderfully written titles from some of today's best authors like Veda Boyd Jones, Yvonne Lehman, Tracie J. Peterson, and many others.

When ordering quantities less than twelve, above titles are $2.95 each.

Hearts♥ng Presents
Love Stories Are Rated G!

That's for godly, gratifying, and of course, great! If you love a thrilling love story, but don't appreciate the sordidness of some popular paperback romances, **Heartsong Presents** is for you. In fact, **Heartsong Presents** is the *only inspirational romance book club*, the only one featuring love stories where Christian faith is the primary ingredient in a marriage relationship.

Sign up today to receive your first set of four, never before published Christian romances. Send no money now; you will receive a bill with the first shipment. You may cancel at any time without obligation, and if you aren't completely satisfied with any selection, you may return the books for an immediate refund!

Imagine. . .four new romances every four weeks—two historical, two contemporary—with men and women like you who long to meet the one God has chosen as the love of their lives. . .all for the low price of $9.97 postpaid.

To join, simply complete the coupon below and mail to the address provided. **Heartsong Presents** romances are rated G for another reason: They'll arrive *Godspeed!*